Glance Gaylord

# Gilbert Starr and His Lessons

Glance Gaylord

**Gilbert Starr and His Lessons**

ISBN/EAN: 9783337028145

Printed in Europe, USA, Canada, Australia, Japan

Cover: Foto ©Andreas Hilbeck / pixelio.de

More available books at **www.hansebooks.com**

RAINFORD
SERIES

# GILBERT STARR

AND

## HIS LESSONS.

BY

GLANCE GAYLORD,

AUTHOR OF "THE BOYS AT DR. MURRAY'S."

BOSTON:

GRAVES AND YOUNG,

No. 24 CORNHILL.

1867.

# Gilbert Starr,

SYMPATHIZE WITH HIM AS HE FINDS HIMSELF LED INTO
CAPTIVITY BY

## PRIDE AND AMBITION,

AND

REJOICE WHEN HE STRUGGLES OUT INTO A BETTER FREEDOM,

THE AUTHOR

### Dedicates this book to them;

HOPING, ALSO,

THAT IF SUCH EFFORTS ARE NEEDED, THEY WILL NOT FAIL
TO MAKE THEM IN THEIR OWN BEHALF.

# CONTENTS.

CONTENTS.

## CHAPTER X.

## CHAPTER I.

### RAINFORD BOYS.

A PLEASANT half-holiday they were having at Mr. Winterhalter's school that afternoon,—pleasant for more reasons than one. In the first place, it was sweet, calm summer weather, which was very enjoyable, and they were having all kinds of games on the lawn; and, added to this, was a pleasant consciousness that Mr. Winterhalter's eyes for once were absent, the master of the Rainford School being called suddenly to a distant town. Half-holidays, too, were no common occurrences, and this made the unusual pleasure a great deal sweeter.

Now, this lawn where the Rainford boys were playing was a very large and pleasant one, though the boys were forbidden to pass beyond the low thorn hedge which marked the play-ground, and just beyond this boundary it sloped broad and green and lovely to the river-edge, — the great, placid river which cut Rainford town in halves, and bore its freights to the sea. Across the river, directly opposite Mr. Winterhalter's, the land rose abruptly, and prominent among the clustered dwellings was a great building which towered, with its many stories, above all the rest. This was a rival boarding-school for boys, so that Mr. Winterhalter's young gentlemen, when at play on their lawn, could see the pupils of the great school over the river run and leap, and even hear them shout over their cricket. A bright, pleasant out-look it was from this sunny lawn, with a wide view of the still, deep river, dotted with sails and pleasure-boats; the little picturesque boat-houses in the shadow of the steep hill; the narrow river-road, winding along the bank, where the drays and lumber-wagons crept along all day, and the hill-side itself, with its great school building, its waving foliage, and its shining roofs and towers.

And as Gilbert Starr, and a half-dozen of the other large boys of Mr. Winterhalter's school, came out of the gymnasium that afternoon, they stopped on the lawn to look at the bright scene before them. Not that they cared particularly for its beauties, nor did they discover any new object of admiration, but at that moment they were thinking of Professor Roth's boys, over the river.

" I declare," said Gilbert, as they paused, " I don't believe, after all, that Roth's boys get any more half-holidays than we do. They havn't had one to my knowledge this term, while we've had one — two — three. Is it two or three, Albert?" he asked, turning to the boy nearest him.

" Two," said Albert Turner.

" And this will be the third," said Gilbert; " now I say Mr. Winterhalter is a clever fellow, anyhow!"

Albert Turner laughed, and said, " Gilbert's wonderfully fond of Mr. Winterhalter since he gave permission to challenge the Roths.  I wonder how long it will last?"

" Till I get into trouble again, I suppose," said Gilbert; " which, by the way, I've resolved not to do this term.  I've turned over a new leaf."

The boys laughed at the idea of Gilbert Starr's turning over a new leaf, and loitered on the steps, hardly knowing what to do with themselves.

Gilbert's was a frank, pleasant face, with great gray eyes, which could look grave or merry, just as their owner chanced to feel. He was the tallest of all the boys, and their acknowledged leader. Whatever Gilbert Starr said or did, Mr. Winterhalter's boys thought was right. They emulated his feats in the gymnasium; they strove to imitate his manly bearing; the Boating Club made him their captain; the little boys brought him their disputes to settle; and there he was, — not yet sixteen, — ruling a miniature kingdom of his own.

How this came about, no one could really tell. Even Mr. Winterhalter was puzzled to know why Gilbert should be so popular. He always seemed to have his own way, and to compromise with no one; and yet that way the majority were always sure to pronounce

right. So the principal concluded that the
boy was one of those persons who are " born
to rule," and congratulated himself that Gilbert took it into his head to lead his followers into nothing that was very bad. Yet
Gilbert's ruling was far from right; and it
was not much wonder that one who felt himself looked up to as a model, whose sway no
one disputed, whose word was law among
the small boys, should grow proud and self-
ish, — though it was all hidden under pleasant ways, so that no one suspected its presence. True, Gilbert never did anything
very bad, — nothing that was shocking or
fraught with great evil, — yet he never used
his great power for good.

Now, as he and his comrades loitered on
the steps, watching those who were at play,
he exclaimed, " Come ! don't let's waste all
the afternoon. Get your pen and ink, Albert, and we'll all go down under the ash

tree, and draw up the challenge. It ought
to be sent over in two or three days, for
they'll want a while to think of it, most likely, and a week or two for practice, and it
will be a month before the race comes off!"

Leaving Albert Turner to go after his
writing materials, the boys sauntered away
in the direction of the great ash tree, which
spread its shadow over one fourth of the
lawn. As they came around the corner of
the piazza which fronted Mr. Winterhalter's
study, Gilbert caught sight of some one sitting in the shadow of the syringa bushes, and
exclaimed, " Who in creation is this?"

The boys stopped to look. A pale-faced
boy sat there, — a boy three or four years
younger than Gilbert, — looking very sad
and homesick, and much as if he had been
crying. He was a slender, slight little
fellow, and shrank from the gaze of the cool,
curious eyes which were bent upon him.

"I say, who's this?" Gilbert repeated, moving nearer the stranger; "a new boy, eh! What's your name?"

At that instant some one tugged at Gilbert from behind. It was little Ned Rogers, the smallest boy in school.

"I can tell you what his name is," said he, in a whisper; "it's Perry Kent, and he's just come, and he's *awful* homesick; and he hasn't any father or mother either, Mrs. Winterhalter told me; and she said I was to play with him, but I can't get him to play a bit. Won't you tell him he's to get up and run about?"

Just then Albert Turner came up with his pens and paper, — Albert was secretary of the Boating Club, — and Gilbert turned away with his friends to the ash tree. *He* couldn't stop to say a comforting word to the little homesick fellow, — how could he? — with so much important business to be done, and all waiting for him to do it! and besides, the idea of such a thing never once entered his head.

From under the ash tree there was a splendid out-look on the river, and the yard of Professor Roth's school, and while these principal members of the Boating Club sat there in conference, they saw the boys of that school come out for intermission.

"Well," said Gilbert, looking at them, "we'll show the Riverside boys what we can do with boats in a few weeks. How do you get on with the challenge, Albert?"

The secretary, who was busy with his pen, replied that the document was not yet ready for criticism, and resumed his scribbling.

"And oh, there's another thing!" cried Gilbert; "Mr. Winterhalter said, just before he went away this noon, that if every boy in the first class would have perfect lessons for the next three weeks, he would offer

a splendid new flag for a prize to the win-
ners. Isn't it nice of him? Professor Roth
can do no less next year."

The secretary looked up from his paper to
say, laughingly, " Mr. Winterhalter knows
his purse won't suffer much. The first class
can't go three weeks with perfect lessons
every day."

" That's so!" said Tom Fowler, who was
the greatest rogue and the dullest scholar in
school; " I can't get perfect lessons a week;
so there goes our chance for a flag!"

" Shame on you!" said Gilbert, impatiently; " you're the greatest dunce, Tom!
— and to have to lose the flag on account of
your dull brains!— I wish you were in the
primary department, learning your A-B-
C's!"

" Then what would you do for an oarsman?" asked Tom, with a twinkle of the
eye, for he was a capital hand at rowing.

"Well, we can't get along without you, that's a fact," Gilbert admitted; "and if we get the flag at all, somebody's got to help your dull wits, I suppose. Come, I'll carry double for three weeks, if you'll only try to help yourself a little; and between us both, perhaps, you can manage to squeeze through without a failure."

"I'll help him with his arithmetic lessons," said Ray Hunter, who was fond of that study.

"But the Latin!" exclaimed Tom, with a hopeless face.

"Gilbert and I will manage that," said the secretary.

"And I'll look up the answers to the history questions," said Barry White.

"There!" said Gilbert, "between us all, I should think we might draw this great hulk of a fellow, even if he hasn't got any brains of his own.   What an easy time Tom 'll have of it for the next three weeks !"

" Not so very easy, if you're all going to poke fun at me like that !" said Tom, grumblingly.

" But what if Mr. Winterhalter should find it out?" said Ray Hunter; " we should all be in disgrace then, and lose the flag besides, most likely."

" Pshaw !" cried Gilbert; " I'll take all the responsibility.   Mr. Winterhalter needn't trouble himself *how* the lessons are got, so long as they're perfect.   And if there's any punishment to bear, I'll take it."

This was one of the little speeches which made Gilbert popular, and this was where he used his influence for wrong.   Had he made the least remonstrance against breaking the principal's rules, the boys would have acquiesced; but, instead, he used his power to further a bad plan.

Here the secretary picked up his papers, saying, " Now be still a minute, will you? Here is the challenge, ready to be copied, and I want your opinion. What a racke* those little chaps are making !   Now listen :


'RAINFORD, East-Side, July 10th.

' The members of the East-Side Boating Club challenge the members of the Riverside Club to race on the river, two weeks from the date of this note, — the challenged to use their new boat " Mermaid," and the challengers to row their new boat " Triton." An early reply is solicited.

' Respectfully,

' ALBERT TURNER,

' Sec. E. S. Boating Club.' "


The secretary folded his paper, and waited for comments.  The rest of the boys looked at Gilbert, and waited also.

" Well," said he, after a few minutes of reflection, " I like that, Albert.  It's short, and to the point, and that's what we wanted."

" You don't say anything about the flag," said Barry White.

" Of course not!" said Gilbert, " we'll wait till we're sure of it, I reckon.  Now, how does that suit you, boys?"

The boys announced their satisfaction.

" Then," said Gilbert, " it's all right, Mr. Secretary, and you can send it over to the Riverside Club just as soon as you choose. And when you get an answer, just let us know.  And tell Mr. Winterhalter, will you, that we're going to try for that flag! You can see him this evening, after he gets back."  And with that, Gilbert jumped up, saying, " I can't stay here 'another minute. There's a dozen things I was to do this afternoon, and not one of them done yet!" And off he walked, followed by his friends.

A half-dozen little boys met him before he had gone far, clamoring loudly about marbles, and the way they had been cheated by an older boy; but Gilbert drove them away, saying, "I can't 'tend to you now! — you're forever quarrelling. Go away, the whole of you!"

His next interruption was from Ray Hunter. "Look there," said he, pointing to the syringa bushes, and pulling Gilbert's sleeve, "that little chap's in trouble. They're plucking him finely!"

Gilbert looked, and saw a clamorous crowd of boys, of all sizes. In the midst of them was the sad-faced little fellow, whom he had previously noticed, and undergoing such torments as only school-boys can devise. A boys' boarding-school is a hard enough place at best, but for timid, soft-hearted little fellows, not old enough nor stout enough to win their way in the great crowd, it is a place of perpetual torment. They are sure to be thrown down in the race, and trampled upon. And little Perry Kent, — timid, shrinking, and just from a dead mother's grave — a mother dead but a week, — had fallen into the hands of the Philistines already. And rare times were the Philistines having with the prize they had captured.

They had robbed him — more in sport at the sight of his terror than anything else — of his knife, a little purse of money, and all the little knick-knacks which they could find in his pockets. These they had distributed among themselves, pretending to the unfortunate victim that he had looked his last on his treasures. They carried him about in their arms, singing mock lullabies, and calling him "Little, precious, darling baby."

They dandled him upon their knees, — as if he were a three-year-old, — and shouted with laughter at the sight of his shame and terror. Some one carried off his hat, and in the confusion one shoe had got lost, or carried off, and there seemed great danger of his being torn to pieces. Just as Gilbert and his party drew near, the largest boys in the crowd were tossing him in the air, — catching the terrified victim, as he descended, in their arms.

# CHAPTER II.

## GILBERT'S PROTEGE.

GILBERT STARR looked on a few minutes in indifference. He had witnessed such scenes a hundred times since he had been at Mr. Winterhalter's. To be sure the principal had expressly forbidden such performances, yet every luckless new-comer, were he a small boy, had to submit to such a merciless initiation. Suddenly he noted how pale the poor victim grew under this ordeal, and something stirred his heart. He could not himself have told what prompted him to interfere.

" Look here!" said he, leaving his follow-

ers, and stepping into the noisy group,
"what are you doing to this little chap?"

"Shaking him up! stirring up his ideas!"
answered the boys, still continuing their sport.

"Well," said Gilbert, coolly, "I advise
you to let him alone."

The boys stopped in astonishment. They
knew Gilbert had witnessed such scenes time
and time again, and never had he offered to
interfere. They doubted their ears. What
could Gilbert Starr care for this puny little
new-comer?

"Why, — why," some of the boys stam-
mered, "what do you mean?"

"I mean," said Gilbert, looking very determined, "that if any of you touch this
little chap again, I'll throw you all into the
river. Do you hear? run away and leave
him alone."

Though this threat was not taken literally,
the crowd saw that Gilbert meant what he

said, and fell back.  Perry Kent, being thus suddenly released from his persecutors, burst into tears, and clung tremblingly to his liberator.

Now, if there was one thing that Gilbert detested more than another, it was a boy that *cried*.  Strong of heart and body himself, — not particularly sensitive to ridicule, — able to cope with the few annoyances he encountered, how could he know or sympathize with tender-hearted Perry's grief?  So he said, rather roughly, — though he was not intentionally unkind, — " Come, little fellow, what are you snivelling about?  Wipe your eyes, and don't be a *baby !*  The boys'll all plague you, if you do like that.  You must get used to 'em."  And, having bestowed this advice, and released himself from Perry's hold, he passed on without further thought of the little boy's troubles.

His comrades began to joke him about the

matter as soon as they had left the unfortunate new-comer behind.

"How came you to do it, Gilbert?" asked Ray Hunter; "I've seen you stand by at such times, when little chaps were getting it harder than this one was, and not lift a finger."

"So have I," said Barry White.

"Well, what of it?" queried Gilbert; "that's nobody's affair. And if I don't choose to see a little fellow tormented to death, who've I to answer to? I'm going up to my room now, and I wish you wouldn't tag. I'll be back in half an hour."

So his followers, being thus curtly dismissed, had nothing to do but throw themselves on the grass, and wait his return.

Little Perry Kent, finding himself alone, sat down under the syringas, and sobbed as if his heart would break. It had been all he could do, when left to himself upon his arrival, to keep back the tears; but now, after what had happened, they flowed unrestrainedly. Only a few short days before, his dear mother had kissed him good-by, and died, and now here was he, — motherless, fatherless, friendless, — alone in this great school, with a disheartening prospect before him. What wonder, then, that the little boy wept, and wished himself dead and sleeping with the dear one whose kind voice and loving, soothing counsel his heart yearned for?

Oh! never so brightly the river might shine on its way to the sea, and the birds sing in the great ash tree, and merrily the boys might be playing all about him, but for them all he had neither eye nor ear. So he sobbed, in his retreat under the friendly shrubs, and no one interrupted his lonely thoughts, till a friendly, freckled face peered in at him, and whispered, " Say ! "

Perry fancied his tormentors had returned, and so did not look up till the voice repeated, " Say ! "

" What ? " said Perry, looking up to see little Ned Rogers standing there.

" Come, don't you cry any more," said the freckled face, " 'tain't good for you, and besides, it's babyish. Why didn't you come and play, as I wanted to have you? then you wouldn't have got tossed up so."

" I can't play, — I don't want to," said Perry, with quivering lips.

" Don't want to play? My ! — but you'll get over that before you've been here long. Oh, but didn't you get off easy, though?" said Ned, exultingly.

" Get off easy?" said Perry, not comprehending.

" Yes ! I mean didn't you get away from those fellows nice ! Why, they'd have tossed you up an hour, perhaps, if that fellow hadn't come along and stopped 'em. They shake boys up dreadfully, sometimes. When I first came here, they almost knocked my breath out of me, and no one offered to stop 'em, either. Oh, but it was lucky for you that Gilbert Starr came along just then!"

" Gilbert who?" asked Perry.

" Gilbert Starr! and he's a splendid fellow. He's the tallest in school, and the smartest, and everybody likes him, and he can beat everything at cricket! When *he* tells anybody to stop a thing, they have to do it, I can tell you! He's just like a king, here; but he's a real good one, and I like him."

" Does he *always* do right?" asked Perry, forgetting his tears.

" Of course he does!" answered Ned, whose ideas of right and wrong were somewhat limited, " and you may think yourself lucky that he took so much notice of you. He never did such a thing for me, anyhow."

Perry felt very grateful, and wiped his eyes.

"Now," said the freckled face, "where's your shoe?"

The new-comer looked down at his feet, and was aware for the first time that one of his shoes was gone. His face grew sad again.

"Well, don't you mind," said Ned, good-naturedly, "I'll look it up. Guess 'tain't far off!" And after searching on the lawn and under the shrubbery, he brought back the shoe to its grateful owner.

Perry put it on, and found his hat near by, under the syringas.

"How long are you going to stay?" Master Ned now ventured.to inquire.

This brought all the lonely thoughts back.

"Oh, dear!" said Perry, almost brokenheartedly, " I've got to stay here a great while, I suppose, — till — till I'm a great, grown boy."

" That ain't so very bad," said Ned, consolingly; " I think it's a splendid place to live. Just see how pleasant 'tis down towards the river'; and we have boat-races every summer; and we can. see the big boys row at sundown, and there's lots of things to see and do, and the boys are first-rate when you get acquainted with 'em. Oh! I think it's a great deal better than home!"

The new-comer looked at, the glittering river, and the emerald slope, and the hill-side beyond, with its clustering dwellings, but saw them all through such sad eyes, that nothing looked beautiful.

Ned's eyes followed, and he said, " That's Mr. Roth's. great boarding-school that you see on the hill, but it isn't so pleasant as this. Their cricket ground don't begin with ours, and then they havn't got a fellow half so smart as our Gilbert Starr. Oh, you'd ought to see him in a boat, or at the bat! Their fellows can't begin!"

By this time Perry began to feel somewhat in awe of the wonderful Gilbert.

"Doesn't he ever plague the little boys?" he asked.

"*He?* No, indeed!" said Ned. "He's above that, I can tell you. He don't look at us very often. But don't sit here any longer. The afternoon's 'most gone, and you havn't played a bit, nor got acquainted with the boys. It's supper time at six o'clock; that'll be here before long. Ain't you hungry? Come, now, we'll go out on the lawn with the rest."

But Perry shrank back, fearful. He hardly wished to make further acquaintance with his schoolmates.

"Oh, don't you be afraid!" said Ned,

confidently; "nobody 'll dare touch you, now that Gilbert Starr's told them not. Come on; you've got to, some time."

This was true, and Perry felt that it might as well be now as any time; accordingly he followed his good-natured friend, with much inward shrinking and reluctance.

Gilbert Starr came down from his room, and found his comrades waiting his appearance.

"I'd ought to go down to Rainford this very minute," said he, "and get some paper and pencils; but there's Tom's lessons for to-morrow staring me in the face,—every one of them a failure, unless he has help. So I move that we get the poor fellow's books, and look out the answers to the questions, and set him at his task. What say you, Tom?"

"It's going to be awful tedious work, having perfect lessons every day for three weeks," said Tom, with a doleful countenance.

The boys laughed.

" You won't have the worst of it, by any means," said Albert Turner, " for we've got to lift you by main strength over the whole long stretch of lessons. I declare! it's as much as the boat-race is worth, anyhow."

" That's so," said Ray Hunter.

" But there's no help for it," said Gilbert, " for Tom's in the first class, and we can't make it otherwise. So get your books, old fellow, and let us get at the work. Albert, you and I will take his translations, Ray shall solve his problems, and Barry, there, can have the questions in history. I'm thankful Tom don't have any more studies. If he had as many as you, Ray, it would be impossible to get him through. How fortunate that Mr. Winterhalter isn't at home this after-.

noon. We shall have to look sharp, boys, when he gets back."

Pretty soon Tom returned from the school-room, and threw his books on the grass, apparently glad to get rid of the trouble of carrying them.

" Good riddance to 'em," said he, " and I wish I'd never got to look in them again."

The party on the grass divided the books among themselves, and, with paper and pencils — which Tom had the forethought to bring — set to work, while he nonchalantly looked on.

Around them the fair, sweet sunshine — getting low and level — fell on the short, rich grass ; a cool breeze sprang up, to sigh about them, and whisper of coming even-tide. Far below, white sails danced and fluttered, and boats dropped down with the tide toward the sea. The echo of shouts floated over from where the Riverside boys were enjoying cricket after school; and just then it seemed the brightest and cheeriest spot on the wide earth.

Gilbert was the first to get through, and pushed away books and work with a sigh of satisfaction that it was done, and sat silently regarding the pleasant stir and life about him. Everything and everybody were very joyous and happy, he thought, and this bustling, active life was well worth living. Tom had at last fallen asleep, and, his other friends being hard at work, Gilbert got up and walked away across the play-ground, thinking he would see whether Mr. Winterhalter had returned.

The little boys were making great noise and clamor in the ground beyond, and just as Gilbert came around the piazza-corner there was a hurried rush of feet, mingled with shouts of laughter and sport, and a little figure, fleeing from its pursuers, ran plump into him.  The shock of collision would have knocked the little boy backward, had not the larger one caught him in his arms; and there the fugitive clung with all his strength, as if it were his only refuge.

"Oh, don't let them get me!  don't let them get me!" cried he, in a voice which could be none other than Perry Kent's.

Gilbert was vexed.  He disliked little boys very much, and to have this one thrust upon him twice in one afternoon was more than he chose to bear.  Some very harsh, contemptuous words were on his lips, but at that instant Perry looked up so pleadingly and so sorrowfully, that they were not uttered.  With that, Gilbert turned to the boys.

"Look here, Copp," said he, to the leader of Perry's pursuers, "did you hear what I told you this afternoon?"

Sam Copp hung his head, and fell back.

"I declare!" said Gilbert, hotly,—in reality more angry because his commands had been disobeyed, than because of Perry's persecution,—"I've a good mind to thrash you soundly! I would, if this little chap weren't hold of me! Now, look here, every boy of you! If you touch him, or trouble him again, I'll take the whole of you at once, and see whether I'll be bothered this way. Do you understand? He's under my care now, and whoever plagues him will have to answer to me!"

The boys moved away, muttering and wondering, leaving Perry and his champion together. Gilbert unclasped the little boy's hands, and put him down on the walk.

"Crying, are you?" said he, looking very much disgusted; "come, don't be such a miserable little baby! Why didn't you turn around, and use your fists on those fellows? But they won't touch you again,

so you can dry your eyes and run about
as much as you please. If they do touch
you, I'll duck 'em all. Now, don't run
into me again, nor let me see you crying
for the next six months," and with that he
started to pass by. But Perry clung to
him, — clung so tenaciously, and with such
an appealing look, that Gilbert was forced
to stop, biting his lips with vexation.

"I'm in for it now," he said to himself;
"I've got this little, whimpering baby fastened to me, to pay for giving him a lift.
O, botheration! I wish I'd let the boys
eat him up, first." Then aloud, —

"Come, what're you hanging on to me
for? I'm in a hurry. I — I — confound
it! if you ain't crying again! Now, look
here," said Gilbert, looking as threaten-
ingly out of his gray eyes as possible, "if
you don't stop your whimpering I'll carry
you straight back to the boys, and tell 'em

to eat you alive for all I care. Do you hear? Now, what do you want of me?"

Perry released his hold, and sat down resignedly on the grass. Something in his hopeless, broken-hearted aspect, touched Gilbert's heart more than any tears or entreaties could have done. He began to relent a little. Looking across the lawn to be sure that his comrades were not in sight, he stooped beside the little boy, saying, in what was meant for a comforting tone, —

"You *do* beat the Dutch at crying, but I don't know as you can help it. Come, we'll go and ask Mrs. Winterhalter if she can give a hungry little boy something to eat. I dare say your mother left you some cakes and things, for luncheon, when she went away."

"I haven't any mother," said Perry, tremulously.

"No more have I," said Gilbert, after a pause, in which his tone grew softer; "and haven't you a father?"

"No," Perry said, without looking up.

Gilbert reflected, with arms folded and eyes off on the river. Could it be that his proud heart was actually touched a little by Perry's condition? If it were, he would have been ashamed to confess it, for a vast quantity of false ideas had crept into the boy's brain, prominent among which was the one that all kinds of tender emotions and sympathy were weak and unmanly. *He* never showed them — never! But when he turned about he took Perry's hand without a word, and led him along the winding walk, across the lawn, and straight to his companions. They began to laugh as soon as he came in sight. But Gilbert walked gravely into their midst, saying, —

" Gentlemen, allow me to introduce to you my protege. His name is — really, I don't know what it is, but you will please to treat him with the utmost consideration for my sake. Hold up your head, my boy, and say, ' how d'ye?' to the gentlemen."

This was said with such a fatherly air and tone, that the boys shouted with merriment. Perry began to tremble, lest he had fallen into the hands of Philistines of a larger growth. But, when his friends had done laughing, Gilbert said, in his natural tone, and quite kindly for him,—

" I expect you'll treat this little fellow well, boys, and not make a fag of him. I've taken him under my charge till he gets used to the place a little, and I'll answer for him; and you shall answer to me if he's ill-treated. I'm going to see if

Mr. Winterhalter's got back;—stay here till *I* get back," and off he hurried.

Perry sat down on the grass, with a heart full of gratitude to Gilbert Starr, and here found the first restful moment since his arrival. The boys gave him no particular attention, but began to joke among themselves about Gilbert, and he was left to himself to wonder at and enjoy the fresh, steady breeze blowing off the river;—the deep, dark shadow of the hill, where the sails gleamed like white wings; the glowing, glittering roofs and towers above in the sunshine—and to think it was all very, very beautiful.

# CHAPTER III.

## SEEKING A RESTING PLACE.

MR. WINTERHALTER was a kindly-looking, bald-headed man, with bushy whiskers streaked with gray. He sat at the head of the supper-table that night, and there Perry Kent saw him for the first time. The boys were seated in the order of their classes, the first class, composed of Gilbert and his friends, sitting nearest the head of the long table, and the other classes in their order. Perry, who as yet belonged to none, would have had a hard matter to find a chair in the long line, had not Gilbert's strong hand again interposed in his behalf, and found him

a seat a little way below himself.   And when
tea was over, and the boys were going back
to finish the holiday on the lawn, Perry had
another experience of his friend's kindness.

"See here," said Gilbert, meeting him in
the door-way, "have you been examined?"

Perry answered, "No."

"Well, come with me, and have it over
with.  'Twon't take long, and then you'll
know what class you're to take, and have
your lessons given to you.  Come, I'll go
with you."

The new-comer gratefully accepted this
invitation, and took Gilbert's offered hand,
confidingly.  "You're *so* good to me!" he
said gratefully, to which Gilbert answered
not a word, but gravely ushered him into
the Principal's pleasant little study.

Mr. Winterhalter was very polite and
kind, and tried to make the little boy feel at
ease.   Gilbert sat down by one of the long

windows and waited, thinking to himself, " Well, this is pretty business for you to be in, Gilbert Starr, marching this little fellow around as if you were his grandfather! You'd better leave him alone."

Just here he heard the Principal say, " What! *you* studying Latin? — well, well! My boys are behind you. And you translate very creditably, my little man. What other studies?"

" Well," thought Gilbert, " if he has studied Latin he can't be so very much of a baby;" and wondered who had been the boy's teacher.

The examination ended at last by putting Perry in the second class — the one below Gilbert's own — and then they went out on the lawn, where Gilbert left his charge to himself while he went off with the Boat Club.

The little boy sat down on the piazza steps, feeling somewhat lighter hearted since sup-

per, and Gilbert's kindnesses. The sun had
gone down — just gone — and there was a
great blaze of light and splendor flaming up
behind the hill; such glory as can only
come after a royal summer day. The tall
cupola on the Riverside schoolhouse, opposite, glowed like a ruddy beacon, and to con-
trast with all the hot, vivid color in the sky,
there was the cool pale green of the foliage
under the hill, the richer emerald of the
great lawn, and the blue of heaven reflected
in the river with the deep, deep, dark
shadows of tower and roof above.

Perry thought he had never seen anything
quite so wonderful and lovely. But soon his
attention was attracted by another sight
which made him forget all about sunset.
The Boating Club came down from their
room,.all ready for their evening practice
upon the river. A gay sight they made, in
their scarlet shirts and loose dark pants, as

they filed across the lawn after Gilbert's lead, and took the little path which wound to the riverside. The boys all crowded around them, following admiringly as far as the hedge would let them go. And when they could follow no farther they huddled beside the thorn-row, shouting hurrahs and praises after the boaters.

"Don't they look smart?" said little Ned Rogers, who spied Perry on the steps, and came to sit down beside him; "our club dresses in red, and the Riverside boys in blue. Blue ain't half so pretty as red, is it?—and our club 'most always beats theirs. Didn't Gilbert look grand and handsome?"

"Yes," said Perry, "he's straight as an arrow."

"You like him, don't you?" said Ned.

"He's been real kind to me," said Perry, gratefully.

"That's so! I tell you I was glad to see

him come around the corner this afternoon
when the boys were after you. I tried to
stop 'em, but my! I couldn't do much; but
when Gilbert took your side they knew what
to expect. Sam Copp won't dare touch you
any more!" at which piece of intelligence
Perry rejoiced.

Master Ned did not find the new-comer
very talkative, but persisted in pressing
acquaintanceship. "Have you been examined? What class are you in? In the
second! Why! I'm way down in the
fourth! Why, where did you learn Latin?
Oh, how smart you be! Won't the boys
stare when they hear of it?" All these
things flowed from the boy's tongue faster
than his new acquaintance could answer
them.

Perry was not very sorry when he
went off, leaving him to enjoy the wide
sweet view, and the sight of the boaters, who

were now afloat and rowing gayly down the river. Not long were they in sight, and when the red figures had quite disappeared from view, the boys came back to their play on the lawn. Perry watched them a great while, till the crimson and purple had faded slowly out of the sky, and a sombre duskiness had settled over river and hill and made them indistinct. A bright star twinkled in the sky, — the same little glittering point which mamma and he had watched together only two short weeks ago. Where was mamma? Oh, in heaven, and so far, far off from him! he thought; and as there is no time like even-tide for sad and home-sick thoughts, back they all trooped to his heart, and he sat silently on the steps, looking at the little golden world on high through swimming tears. Did mamma see it? Did she see *him*, lonely and tearful, on the steps? Did she long to wipe away his tears, and whisper that she saw him and watched over him? Who could tell?

So he sat silently, not daring to sob aloud lest the boys should hear him, yet so grieved and desolate that he laid his head on the steps, and shut his hands tightly over his mouth to smother the cries that trembled on his lips. By and by a bell in a distant part of the building rang a little peal, and the boys slowly began to leave the lawn. They found an entrance at one end of the building, and so Perry was left undisturbed, none coming near enough to notice the little figure hid in the shadow. And when they were all gone, and the lawn was left in dusk and silence, he raised himself up, wondering if it were really bed-time, and why no one told him where to sleep. He wondered whether Gilbert Starr and his Boat Club had returned. He looked up and saw no lights flashing from any of the windows, — all was wrapped in darkness and silence. Only on Riverside the lights gleamed out on the hill, and far down on the river a sparkle of light shone out now and then from some boat-prow. He began to fear that all the inmates of the school were abed and asleep, the house was so silent. From some high steeple on the hill, hidden in the darkness, came nine long sonorous tolls, floating firm and distinct on the stillness. Nine o'clock, — time for all schoolboys to be in bed. Gilbert, he thought, might long ago have returned, and gone to his room without seeing him. What could he do? Sleep on the steps all night? That was not such a terrible matter; but, ah, it was so hard to feel that nobody cared for him! — nobody cared!

Just as he was laying his head down again on the hard step, there floated to his ears broken sounds of talk, — whispers, low laughter, and then the sound of footsteps coming across the lawn. It was the Boat Club. Perry got up joyfully and listened a moment to assure himself of the fact, then ran in the direction of the sound.

" Who's this?" cried Tom Fowler, catching him roughly by the shoulder; " look here, boys, here's the biggest musquito I've seen to-night. Help me despatch him, will you?"

" Who is it, anyway?" said Ray Hunter; " it was time for the under-classes to be in bed half an hour ago."

" I declare," said Tom, " if I don't believe it's Gilbert's protege, though it's so dark I can't rightly see !"

" Is that you, Perry Kent?" asked Gilbert, in a vexed tone.

" Yes, it's me," said Perry, faintly.

" Well, then why aren't you in bed?" asked Gilbert; " only the first class are allowed to be up till nine, and we're a little late. Come, what are you here for, I say?"

Perry's voice trembled as he replied: "I didn't know where to go, and nobody told me anything—and—and—" and here he had to stop.

Gilbert was a trifle out of temper, and replied crossly—"If you aren't big enough to find out, you never will be! But I've got you to look out for, I suppose, so come along and see if we can find Mrs. Winterhalter. It's a pretty time of night to be looking up a sleeping-place."

"Don't be hard with him, Gilbert," said Ray Hunter; "he's only a little fellow, you know, and can't make things go smooth yet."

But Gilbert was out of hearing, hurrying his charge in the direction of Mrs. Winterhalter's parlor. To Perry it seemed as if they made a prodigious noise as they hurried along the empty halls. He was afraid Mr. Winterhalter would come out of his study to see what was the matter. But no one appeared, and when they arrived at the parlor door a bright light shone through the red glass, plainly showing that the lady was within. Gilbert rapped. Mrs. Winterhalter herself opened the door,—a kind motherly woman of fifty; just the sort of person, one would think, to get along with such a great parcel of boys,—and said, with a look of surprise, "Why, this you, Gilbert? Come in, my dear." And they passed in.

"Mrs. Winterhalter," said Gilbert, illy concealing his vexation, "here's this little boy that came to-day hasn't any place to sleep. Where will he be put?"

"Dear! dear!" said the good lady, throwing up her hands; "I forgot *all* about the little fellow. Why, how *could* I?—and he a little motherless boy! Come here, dear, and see me.  Why, you're tired to death, child,— and no where to lay your head.  You thought we were all heathen, here, didn't you?  But Mr. Winterhalter's been away all the afternoon, and there was so much to do that I forgot all about you.  It was wicked in me, I will say!  Thank you a hundred times, Gilbert, for bringing him here."

"But, where will he sleep?"  Gilbert asked, hardly able to conceal his impatience.

The kind-hearted lady left Perry and seated herself at a secretary, turning over great books and talking cheerfully to the little boy all the while.

"What class is he in, Gilbert?" she asked.

"In the second, ma'am."

"In the second!— that little fellow!  Well, well, let me see.  The second class — room  No.  2 — second  story — twenty beds — all full.  Dear!—why, the beds are all full!"

"There are the other class-rooms," suggested Gilbert.

"Crowded already," said the lady, reflectively; "I don't know what we can do, I'm sure.  Mr. Winterhalter keeps taking more pupils, and leaves me to put them somewhere, though I keep telling him there isn't room for another one.  He thinks boys and beds are made of India-rubber, I expect.  That's always the way with men! —But, there, Gilbert, I've just thought!" as a bright idea struck her, "would you mind sharing your bed with him to-night? —just till I can put up a little bed for him somewhere.  The beds in your room are larger, and not crowded at all, you know. I wonder I didn't think of it before!  I know you'll be glad to accommodate the poor motherless little boy."

Gilbert was *not* glad! He was so vexed that he could hardly keep back some hard words. But he silently acquiesced, for the wildest of the Rainford boys would not have inconvenienced kind Mrs. Winterhalter.

"There," said she, in a tone of relief, "now you'll do nicely. Gilbert will be good to you, I know, and to-morrow I'll make everything right. Good night, dear," stroking back his hair as his own mother had done, "go and get some sleep, and you'll feel better;" and with that she ushered them out.

Gilbert led the way up to the long room in which the first class slept, feeling as if he would like to throw his charge out of the first open window which they passed. Poor Perry felt his coldness most deeply, and followed with a heavy heart. His benefactor gave him not a word of kindness or encouragement, and ushered him into the sleeping apartment with a face which was a study. Here the Boat Club, and all the boys of the first class, were leisurely preparing for bed — unlacing their high shoes and removing their uniforms — and some were already asleep. All eyes were turned on Gilbert as he entered.

"Hello!" said Tom Fowler, in amazement, "you haven't brought that little midget to room up here, Gilbert Starr?" and the faces of the rest showed their astonishment.

"Why, it's no place for him!" said Barry White; "why don't he go into one of the other rooms, where he belongs?"

"It's an imposition!" said Tom, grumblingly.

Gilbert sat down on the edge of his bed, without a word, unlaced his shoes, and threw them violently into a corner.

"Gilbert's mad!" said Ray Hunter, who, being Gilbert's warmest friend, presumed to say things which Starr would not have borne from others;—"I know by the way he throws off his shoes. Repent of your bargain, don't you, Gil?"

"*We* shall if he don't, I guess," said Albert Turner; "such little chaps are always a torment, and always under a body's feet."

"If he gets under my feet I'll step on him," said Tom, with a warning look at the "torment."

"Let's put Gilbert and his protege out of the room!" said Bob Upham, who was also a member of the Boat Club.

Perry shrank out of sight as much as possible, thinking, at last, that there was really no place for him in the whole wide earth. Two bright spots on either of Gilbert's cheeks showed that his temper was roused. At last the words came which he would not bear.

"No," said Barry White, in answer to Bob Upham's words, "let's put out the protege, and let Gilbert stay. He's well enough, when he's alone. Come, I say, let's —"

But Gilbert was in the middle of the floor before White could say more, — eyes blazing, and looking defiance at them all.

"I've heard enough," he said slowly, — "all that I will hear from any of you. There's no room for him in any of the other class-rooms, and if I choose to share my bed with him it's no affair of yours. Stay here he's got to, and stay here he *shall*, and if you wish to undertake to put him out — very well."

"Pshaw! we were only joking, Gilbert," said Tom Fowler.

"Joking or not," said Perry's champion,

"I won't hear any more of it," and turned away from them all to his own bed; and, having vented his vexation upon his friends' heads, he began to regard Perry with kindlier eyes.

"You mustn't mind what they say," he said to the little boy, as he threw off his crimson jacket; "they don't hate you half so bad as you think. Come, hurry into bed, for the lights'll be out in a few minutes."

Perry made haste to obey, took the shoes off his tired feet, and, when he was undressed, knelt down on the floor to say his prayers. He had always said them at his mother's knee — always — and, since her absence, had felt her loss most keenly when the time came to thank God for life and health and watchful care. The thought never entered his head that he was doing anything strange or unusual in the eyes of those around him, and he did not suspect that they neglected, or were indifferent to perform, the same duty. So, with a very quiet face, he knelt there before them all, only feeling in his weary heart that it was a very sweet and comforting thing to do, and that perhaps mamma looked down, too, and was pleased.

Gilbert did not notice him till he turned about to see whether the boy had obeyed his order, and gone to bed. The sight half startled him. With a smothered " What!" he turned away, and looked at his companions. They, too, were looking at Perry — some with amazement, some with curious, half-averted faces. Not one of them but what had once knelt at his mother's knee, but since coming to school — ah, it had been very different. In truth, they were ashamed to pray before one another. Even Gilbert, who confessed no fear of any one, would have thought it savored of weakness and unmanliness to have got down upon his knees to pray; — being, plainly, ashamed to do it. As if it could be weak or unmanly to tell one's wants, and crave the love and care of Him who holds our very lives in his hand! But that was an evil way of thinking which the Rainford boys had got.

When Gilbert turned back, Perry had finished his prayer, and was nestling down among the pillows with a sigh of weariness, or sorrow, he could not tell which; and Gilbert followed him, thinking, —

" Well, he's a queer little fellow; but they sha'n't plague him for it, anyhow."

# CHAPTER IV.

## SUNDAY AFTERNOON.

ALBERT TURNER, the Boating Club's secretary, carried the challenge over to the secretary of the Riverside School. And then the Rainford Club waited impatiently for an answer.

Much ado they had to get Tom Fowler's lessons for him, and yet keep the fact a secret from Mr. Winterhalter. Somehow these boys had very perverted ideas of honor. Gilbert Starr, who would have scorned to tell a falsehood — to have played his friends false — to have done a cowardly or mean thing, — all because it was not *honorable*, yet, day after day, worked at Tom's translations, and deceived Mr. Winterhalter into believing that that study-hating youth was very attentive and industrious all at once. And, while engaged in this difficult and tedious process of " cramming " the dullest member of the class, the thought that there was anything wrong or dishonorable about it never once entered his head. Had this method of gaining the coveted flag been called " dishonest," the boys would have resented it at once. It was only " fooling," or " giving Tom a lift," or " pulling wool over Winterhalter's eyes," when they had occasion to speak of the matter.

About a week after the boys commenced their strife for perfect lessons, the flag, which Mr. Winterhalter had ordered, arrived. It was a splendid scarlet pennon, with a gold-broidered edge; and when Gilbert saw it fluttering from its slender, silver-tipped ebony staff, he mentally resolved that no pains should be spared but what the flag should become the Club's.

Mrs. Winterhalter was true to her word, and forgot Perry no more. After going again and again through the sleeping-rooms of the different classes, crowding a little here, moving another there, she declared it was no use, — there was room for the new-comer in none of them. So, grumble as much as they would, the first class were obliged to receive him into their room, and a bed was placed for him in an unoccupied corner. Here Perry would have fared but poorly but for the strong protection of Gilbert's favor; and sometimes, in that person's absence, he was subjected to all kinds of tyranny; but those occasions were rare, and the little boy gradually began to like his new situation, as he became more and more acquainted, and at his ease. It was not strange that in these, his first days at school,—enjoying himself only by Gilbert Starr's intervention,—he should come to look upon that person as his best and truest friend, loving him better than a brother, admiring his prowess, his feats in the gymnasium, and happy to receive Gilbert's praise and feel that he felt for him, cared for him, regarded his wants.

As for Gilbert Starr himself, he regarded his charge with a strange mixture of kindness, respect, and dislike, sometimes being extremely kind and gentle with him, again treating him with coldness and neglect. Regarding him as particularly his own property, he would allow none of his comrades to offer him any insult or indignity, or to play the tyrant and make a slave of the little boy. All this was very fortunate for Perry's happiness, and, if treated unkindly or slightingly he had got to be, he much preferred to have it come from Gilbert's hands. And, to tell the truth, it came from his hand quite often enough.

Once, when the Boat Club had strolled far down the river-side, and Perry had received permission to follow, Ray Hunter, who was oppressed by the warmth of the sun, took off his coat, and threw it over the little boy's shoulder, for him to carry. As if the little boy's shoulders were stouter than Ray's own broad and stalwart ones! Gilbert was ahead of his party, and did not notice the fact at first, and Perry struggled on with his double burden, almost sweltering with the heat. But when Gilbert did notice what had oc-curred, he quietly transferred the jacket to his own arm, and walked on without saying a word.

They rambled on and on, enjoying all the fragrance and freshness in the river-meadows, and when they were ready to return, Ray bethought him of his coat. There it was, swinging from Gilbert's arm.

" Gilbert," said Ray, in astonishment, " my jacket, — how came you by it?"

" I found it on a little boy's shoulder," said Gilbert, gravely; "I thought mine could carry it better."

Ray Hunter took his coat with very red cheeks, and after that Perry was troubled with no burdens of other people.

The first Sabbath after the little boy's arrival was a very bright and sunny one. Mr. Winterhalter's boys attended church but once a day, and that was at morning service. The church was a very pleasant one, standing in a quiet spot in the midst of Rainford streets, and thither the school walked in procession every Sabbath morning, and back at noon. The afternoon was spent at home, and quiet and orderly afternoons they generally were, considering how many turbulent spirits were endeavoring to hold themselves in check.

After the light Sunday-noon lunch that day, Perry had taken his Bible, — worn and smooth with the press of dear mamma's fingers, — and sat down on the farthest corner of the piazza, where the boys did not often come. The syringas shielded him from the sun, and made a cool and pleasant nook. On a far edge of the lawn, by the thorn-hedge, a great many boys were congre-- gated. He did not know how they were spending Sunday afternoon, but now and then faint laughter floated to his ears, and he was pretty sure Sam Copp was telling some of his funny stories, of which he had an inexhaustible store.

Perry turned over leaf after leaf, re-joicing to see where mamma had marked passage after passage, — very comforting passages, too, just suited now to her lonely little boy. Seated here in the quiet and silence, he read and thought of the happy days before mamma went away,— not with tears and regret, but very calmly and peacefully, as something sweet and precious to ponder over. Sometimes he put his book aside to look on the far, far stretch of river,— warm and burnished in the sunshine,— all the boats and sails at rest in their harbors, and the water at rest, too,— only softly lapping the shore, and rustling in the grasses. And the whole earth seemed at rest, and the clouds lay motionless, and there was such sweet, sweet Sabbath stillness over all, that it almost seemed a pity that ever the drays must rattle, and the boatmen shout, and the bustle and clamor reign again.

But Perry's quiet did not last long, for presently Gilbert, and a good many boys of the first class, came down from their room, and sat down on the grass, the other side of the syringas. None of them noticed him.

Gilbert said, as soon as they were seated, " Now, Mr. Secretary, we'll listen to you. I've been wanting to hear it all day, but there wasn't time before church, and this is the first minute I have got to myself since. But when did the reply come? How did you get it?"

" Sure enough," said Tom Fowler; " Professor Roth don't let his boys run about with letters, Sunday."

Here Perry began to understand that they were talking about the reply to the Boat Club's challenge, of which he had heard so much. It shocked him some, for there was Gilbert talking about matters for which Sunday had no place, — talking very coolly and unconcernedly, too, as if it were no unusual thing.

" Well," replied Albert Turner, " here's

the way I came by it: You know I was the last to come in last night, — after you were all abed?"

"Yes," said Gilbert, "I remember."

"Well, just as the bell rang for nine, and you were all starting for your rooms, I heard a whistle at the lower end of the lawn, and went down to see who was there. I couldn't find the fellow at first, it was so dark; but when I did find him, it was one of Roth's boys."

"Which one?" said Ray Hunter.

"Fred Moore," said the secretary

"It takes him to come across the river in a dark night," said Ray, admiringly; "there ain't a fellow in *this* school could do it!"

"Well, Fred Moore it was," continued the secretary, "and he brought this reply. He said Roth had forbidden them to cross the river again this month, so he had to wait till pitch-dark to cross over without being seen.　Here's the reply, if you want to hear it :

'RIVERSIDE, July 14th.

'*Sec. E. S. Boating Club:*

' The members of the Riverside Club accept your challenge to race with the new boats on the river, three weeks from July 10, and Captain Forrest, of our Club, wishes to meet Captain Starr, of your Club, on Rainford bridge, next Wednesday night, to make arrangements for the same.　Hoping he will comply, we remain,

' Yours truly,

' RIVERSIDE CLUB.' "

" That sounds like it," said Gilbert, enthusiastically ; " I'll be at Rainford bridge, never fear ! "

" That is, if Mr. Winterhalter will let you go," said Barry White.

" Pooh ! he'll let Gilbert do 'most any-

ANSWER TO THE CHALLENGE.  Page 78.

thing," said Ray; "there'll be no trouble about that. The most I fear, is that we shall lose the flag by some of Tom's blundering. Did you hear him Friday afternoon? Oh, but I thought it was all up with us, then! But he blundered out the right answer, at last, and so saved himself!"

"Well, it's no wonder," said Tom, complainingly; "you never cross your t's, nor dot your i's, nor half write anything. How be I going to know what's what?"

"Guess at it!" returned Ray.

Here a new idea flashed into Perry's mind. The boys were deceiving Mr. Winterhalter, and Gilbert was aiding! It is a hard thing to have the faults of those whom we love and admire thrust upon our knowledge, and Perry was very much startled to find his champion deliberately doing wrong. It both shocked and grieved him.

Then Gilbert said, "If we really *do*

succeed in earning the flag, and Mr. Winterhalter puts it up for the race, we must contrive not to lose it. It would mortify me horribly to have Roth's boys bear it off."

"It would all of us," said Bob Upham, who had just sauntered up; "think how grand Forrest would look, as he went up to receive it."

"We should get laughed at finely for losing our flag in that way," said Barry White; "better lose it, if we must, through Tom's dull wits."

"Look here," said Tom, at this, "if, after we've beat 'em out and out, and got the flag, you'll give me half the credit for my help that you do for my being dull, I'll think myself a lucky fellow."

"Alas! true merit rarely gets its reward in this world," said Ray, shaking his head.

The sun had got around so that it shone

bright, and full, and hot where the boys were sitting. They got up and began to disperse — some going to the ash tree, and some back to their room. Gilbert and Ray Hunter kept on toward the piazza, and here Ray's keen eyes spied Perry. "Look there," he said to Gilbert, "there's your protege. He's been as whist as a mouse all the while we've been talking, and right behind us, too."

"Let's see what he's up to," said Gilbert, going up the steps.

"Well, Perry," said Ray, "here's your grandfather, Gilbert, who takes a warm interest in your affairs. He wants to know what you're doing this hot afternoon."

"I declare! if you aren't reading, — or are you studying your Lexicon?" said Gilbert, sitting down beside him; "why don't you run and sit with the boys, out there? they're having a fine time, I guess."

Perry was silent.

"Yes, why don't you go and tell stories with the boys?" queried Ray; "now for a reason!"

"I don't think it's right to do so," Perry answered, quietly.

"Not right!—why, Mr. Winterhalter don't forbid it!" Ray answered, quickly.

"Oh, I don't mean that," said Perry; "but the Bible tells us not, you know, and God has forbidden it."

A quick smile flashed over Ray Hunter's face, and he turned to Gilbert with a half-puzzled, half-contemptuous look, and said, "Well, that beats all the reasons I ever heard!"

Gilbert said nothing, nor smiled.

"What has He forbidden?" Ray asked, after a little pause.

"Why, one thing is to break Sunday,"

Perry answered; "and it's breaking it to do as they are doing, I thought."

"Is it wrong to laugh?" Ray persisted with mock gravity.

"Why, no," said the boy, hesitating, — "not wrong to laugh I shouldn't think, but I meant it was wrong to do such things as belong to other days, and to talk about work, and — and — boat clubs."

"There!" said Ray, laughing heartily, "we've got it now, Gilbert! Do you understand?"

Gilbert nodded assent.

Just here Bob Upham called to Ray from across the lawn, and he went away, laughing and saying, "Now give Gilbert a good lecture, little fellow! He needs it."

When he was gone, Perry looked up into Gilbert's face to see if he were offended.

Gilbert looked down, smiling, and said —

"Well, begin the lecture, Perry. I'm all attention."

"I've no lecture to give," said Perry, gravely.

"Haven't you a word to reprove me with? Now, little fellow, I want to ask you a question. Were you in earnest in what you said just now?"

"In *earnest?* To be sure I was!" said his protege, wonderingly.

"And you think it's wrong to laugh, and tell stories, and talk about business and boat clubs on Sunday, do you?"

"Yes," softly, but confidently.

"And you think, too, that I'm a bad boy for doing it, don't you?"

Perry hesitated. It was hard to think anything bad of Gilbert, and he such a friend,— yet he answered, though somewhat timidly,—

"Yes, I think it was wrong."

" Bravo !" said Gilbert, not at all dis-
pleased, and secretly admiring his little
friend for his frank courage; " and now what
are you going to do about it?"

" I can't do anything but be sorry. I
wish I could."

" Well, now what in the world are you
sorry for? What difference does it make
with you?"

" Because — because — I love you, and
hate to have you do wrong and be wicked,"
Perry timidly answered.

Gilbert was silent so long after this, that
the little boy looked up to see if he was
angry. No, — he was only looking at the
wide, still sweep of river — burning, flashing, sparkling — and his gray eyes looked
their softest. So he took heart.

" Well," said Gilbert, at last, " how have
*you* been spending Sunday? Perhaps, if you

tell me, I shall know how to do the same thing sometime."

" I've been reading the Bible, and thinking a little, — and — and that's all, since I came from church," said Perry; " when mamma was alive, I had my verses to say, and she could talk beautifully to me."

" And, now you're all alone, you keep Sunday by yourself," said Gilbert. " Well, you're a queer chick! Why, we think Sunday is the dullest and tiresomest day in the whole seven. Now don't you?"

" I don't think this is dull or tiresome," said Perry; " I've got this Bible, and there's the long wide river to look at, and all the pleasant things down on the shore and over on Riverside."

" So this is your Bible, is it?" said Gilbert, taking up the book; " really, but I thought it was your Lexicon. And, now I think of it, how came you to pray before all the boys, the other night? Weren't you afraid?"

"*Afraid!*" said Perry, again opening his eyes to their widest extent, "why, who could hurt me?"

"No one;—I only meant weren't you afraid the boys would see you, and laugh, or something?"

"Why, no," said Perry, wonderingly again; "don't the boys pray, too?"

Gilbert gave him a sudden keen look from out his gray eyes, and answered, "No, not one of them."

"What! not *you?*" cried Perry, shrinking back.

The crimson color came into Gilbert's cheeks, then slowly faded out. "No, Perry," he said quite gravely, "not I."

The little boy's face showed how much he was shocked and disappointed, and Gilbert, who saw it, felt strangely embarrassed. It was only a little boy — not worth minding — yet, somehow, it was not pleasant to feel that he had fallen in his estimation.

And all he said seemed so fresh and simple! — so free from art, and hypocrisy — "just as if he believed it all, and loved it," Gilbert said to himself, — that he had listened to much, which, from other lips, he would not have paid heed.

And, after a long silence, during which several voices had called to him from the lawn, he got up from the steps, picked up Perry in his strong arms, saying, " So I'm a great deal worse than you thought me for, am I? Well, that's too bad. I'm not a good fellow, at all; I don't pretend to be. Didn't you know it? couldn't you see it? But we may be pretty good friends, after all, I guess," putting his protege down again; — " only," he added, laughingly, " I must go and break Sunday a little more."

Perry watched him as he walked slowly and erect—proud, strong, handsome—back to his comrades, and sighed and wondered what he could do to make Gilbert love the Right better than the Wrong.

And the long afternoon came to a close with soft puffs of wind from down the river; with violet shadows under the emerald hillside; with rosy streaks and stains of color over all the sky, and this was Perry's last thought that night, — " If Gilbert only loved Right better than Wrong !"

# CHAPTER V.

## ABOUT THE FLAG.

NOW that the Riverside Club had accepted their challenge, Gilbert and his boys
renewed their exertions to win the flag; and,
with getting Tom Fowler's lessons for him,
and long evenings of practice upon the river,
the remainder of July was a busy season.

Captain Starr went down to Rainford
Bridge one evening, at twilight, and had the
desired interview with Captain Forrest. The
two boys were nearly of a height, each
the tallest and strongest of their respective
schools, and, being the pride and boast of
their school-fellows, and the frequent cause

of collisions between them, the two had become strong rivals. They had a very peaceable interview, however, on the Riverside end of the bridge,—Captain Forrest's school having been forbidden to cross the river,—and the two captains parted with a mutual respect for each other; one secretly apprehensive that the other would gain the victory.

Gilbert went back to school, vowing that his club should go into harder practice than ever, to make success certain; and Captain Forrest resolved much the same thing, as he slowly climbed the hill to his own school-grounds.

" I tell you what," Gilbert said, as he returned, a little after dusk, and found Ray Hunter waiting for him, " I like that Forrest! He's a bully fellow, and means what he says; and Ray, old fellow, we'll have to stir ourselves if we beat his club. You see,

they're all as fond of him as they can be,
and · mind every word he says, and he *is*
posted in boating."

So it came about that Captain Starr's best
men were out on the river every pleasant
evening, after that, from the earliest moment
after supper, till the latest moment which
they dared to be absent after nine o'clock.
Had not Mr. Winterhalter been quite lenient,
and looked upon their boating-practice with
a favoring eye, the belated club would often
have found themselves locked out, as they
returned home long after the bells had
chimed for nine.   But, somehow, the back
hall-door was always unlocked, however late
they came, and they stole softly up to their
room without reproval; till, taking advantage — as boys will — of this leniency, they
failed to make their appearance till ten was
trembling upon all the bells in Rainford,

and that night they found Mr. Winterhalter waiting for .them with a very grave face.

"It seems I can hardly trust to my boys' honor," he said, as they trooped into the hall.

"Honor, sir?" said Gilbert, with a flushed face, as he stood at the head of his companions.

"Yes, honor," said Mr. Winterhalter; "I have favored you somewhat of late, I believe. Is this the way in which I am to be repaid? After this, young gentlemen, you will return at precisely nine o'clock; any variance from this rule will be a sufficient cause for a fall from your class-rank. Good-evening." And the. Principal disappeared.

The boys went up to their rooms.

"Now we are in for it," said Ray, with a melancholy face; "that means that we're to start for home as soon as half-past eight."

"A great time for practice that will leave," muttered Tom.

"Well, we can't help ourselves," said Gilbert, resignedly; "we shouldn't have been such fools as to take advantage of Winterhalter.　Don't you know it?"

"I don't see how it's dishonorable, anyhow," said Barry White.

"Neither did I, at first," said Gilbert; "but if you allow that we took the advantage of him, you'll have to confess that it's — well — not the fair thing."

"A bother on such fine distinctions!" grumbled Tom; "I get enough of 'em from that little chap in the corner, out there, without hearing any from you, Cap'n Starr."

"That's so!" said Bob Upham.　"What do you think he had the impudence to tell me, the other day?"

"Getting saucy, is he?" said Tom; "I'll put a stop to that."

"I don't believe Perry was ever impudent to one of you," said Gilbert, looking at the little boy, as he lay sleeping peacefully in his corner.

"Then I'll convince you," said Bob. "The other night, when you went down to meet Forrest on the bridge, you know you left Tom's confounded old Latin lesson for me to work out. Well, I was hot and tired, and didn't want to touch it; so I said to this little chap—you know he beats the Dutch at Latin—'Come, little chap, I'll give you a dime to look out this page for me.'

"'I'll do it for nothing, if I can,' said he, as sweet as sugar. So I gave him the book and paper in a jiffy, and happened to say, 'Now do it right, or Tom'll blunder, and there 'll be an end of our flag.'

"You'd ought to have seen the young-un's face; it was as long as a parson's.

"'What on earth's the matter?' I cried out; and if you'll believe me, he had the impudence to tell me to my very face that it was wrong to look out Tom's lessons for him; that it was deceiving the Principal, and all that sort of thing, and he couldn't do it for me, and, if you'll believe it, I couldn't make him!"

"Why didn't you chuck him out the window?" said Tom.

"Well, I thought if I did that I should have Gilbert about my ears, so I kept my hands off him; but I thought I'd let him know that Gil wa'n't so much nearer perfection than the rest of us, so I said, 'Come, now, what are you thinking about? Gilbert Starr does it, too, and you think he does everything about right.'"

"What business had you to tell him what I do?" queried Gilbert, impatiently.

"Beg your pardon," said Bob; "it was all for the sake of getting the Latin lessou done; so don't grumble."

"Well, what did the little lamb say, when you told him that?" asked Tom.

"Oh, he said that he knew Gilbert did wrong, and so on, and I gave up trying to do anything with the little mule, and had to do all the translations myself. Now if that was not the height of impudence!"

But the boys were nearly all in bed, and Gilbert blew out the lamp, leaving Bob to get in in the dark. Not that he himself had gone to bed, or was ready to; he sat at the foot of it, thoughtfully unlacing his shoes. Why was it that a little feeling of discontent had crept into his heart? Not discontent with school, his studies, his friends, his pleasures, nor his prospects, — then what?

Himself? Gilbert could not tell; it was the problem which he was trying to solve. It was not a very troublesome sensation as yet, only a faint sense, down in his heart, that something was not as it should be; who, or what it might be, he did not know. Perhaps it was only an increased thoughtfulness, which perceived things amiss whose evil had not been imagined before. At any rate, he sat at the foot of his bed a long time after the boys were asleep, gravely thinking of some things which the little boy in the corner had said, and unconsciously judging himself by their standard; wondering, too, why he so much disliked to have the little fellow aware of his wrong-doing. Why should *he* care what that little chicken thought or said? —*he*, the tallest, smartest boy in school, and the ruler of it! Why, if he chose, he could prevent that little fellow reading his Bible, stop his tongue, and forbid him to do what he thought was right.  And why not?

Gilbert went to bed, saying to himself, "You'd better look out, Gilbert Starr, and let such thoughts alone; they'll do you no good.  If you keep on, you'll get to be a great baby and a muff, and then you'll be a fine sight.  Better stick to your old ways, and look out for your boating and things."  And so, with a sigh, he went to sleep, and put away thoughts which perplexed him.

After this, matters went on prosperously with the Boat Club.  Gilbert brought them back to their room by nine o'clock, every evening, and in so doing won Mr. Winterhalter's favor again.  And as the time drew nearer and nearer for the expiration of the three weeks, not only those directly interested, but the whole school, waited anxiously to see whether the flag was to be won.

It was now necessary to prepare Tom

Fowler's lessons with a great deal of care
and secrecy; and, to prevent mistakes, Gilbert generally took the precaution to look
over all the prepared lessons before they
went to Tom; so, with his own to get, and
with long hours of practice on the river, his
were no idle days.

It was quite natural that Mr. Winterhalter
should be surprised at the ease with which
Tom seemed to master his lessons. He had
formerly been the dullest scholar in the
class; but this unusual smartness failed to
excite any suspicious in the principal's
mind. He thought to himself that his previous dulness must have been owing to the
lack of a motive for studying, or from sheer
laziness; and that, now that he had an in-
centive, he had proved himself capable of
doing as well as any one.

But it all came to an end at last,—the
toil, hard study, deception and fraud,—

and the class were victors. Three weeks of perfect lessons ! it was something unprecedented in school annals. Gilbert took up his books at the close of recitations on the last afternoon, with a thrill of pride that the class had been successful. What a zest it would add to the race ! How both clubs would strain all their energies, the one to retain, the other to possess it ! His cheeks glowed, and his eyes sparkled as he thought of it. Then, like a dash of icy water, crept that disagreeable sensation into his heart. Was it deception they had practised to gain the flag? Was there no softer name for it? Was it strictly honorable, to say nothing about the right and wrong of the subject? He was in no mood to think of these things, and crushed them back as best he could, and just then Mr. Winterhalter came in with the superb pennon.

"Here," said he to Gilbert, who was al-

ways supposed to represent the class, " take
the flag, boys;  it is well earned.    I hope
you'll have a fine day for the race, to-morrow, and see to it that you don't dishonor
your flag."

The boys cheered a little at this.    Then
Gilbert stood up, and said, in behalf of his
class, —

" We thank you for it, Mr. Winterhalter,
and hope we may deserve it;" and added,
" Will you allow us to put it up for the race,
to-morrow?"

"Certainly," said Mr. Winterhalter; "the
flag is yours;  do with it as you choose,
though I certainly hope that our Boat Club
may be so successful as to retain it this side
the river."

"That we will!"   "Good for you!"
"Hurrah for Mr. Winterhalter!" cried the
boys, as they filed out of the recitation-room
with Gilbert, who carried the flag.

Out to the lawn they went, and the pennon was stuck up under the ash tree, where the whole school might see it. The boys of the lower classes received it with applause, and gave the Boat Club such a round of cheers that it echoed, and re-echoed, and floated across the river to the ears of the Professor's boys, who faintly returned it.

"Now, three cheers for Captain Starr!" shouted Rufe Fitch, who was the head-boy of the second class; and three such cheers were given as would have gratified the heart of any boy.

Gilbert received them very pleasantly, as he was wont to do all such signs of his popularity, and drawing a long sigh, said to Ray Hunter, —

"I'm glad I've got Tom Fowler off my shoulders."

"Yes, he *is* a heavy fellow," said Ray, "it's been about all the whole of us could

do to carry him; but think how he'll handle an oar, to-morrow!—that pays for the
trouble he's been."

Gilbert shook his head, as if he were not
quite sure of the fact. "I don't know;—
I wish I did," he said, presently; "I've
thought that—that—perhaps we'd better
have run the risk of losing Tom, and getting
beat in the race, than to carry on this under-
handed business about the lessons."

Ray Hunter faced his friend, quickly,
saying, "Gilbert Starr, you're a—" The
epithet "fool" trembled on his lips, and
though it was not uttered, Gilbert understood what was meant.

"It wouldn't do for every one to say
that," he remarked, quietly.

"That's so, Gilbert,—forgive me; but
you *do* get some outrageous notions into
your head, lately. And it's all because of
that Perry Kent, I'm thinking. Now look

here, old fellow," laying his hand on Gilbert's shoulder, " you know I love you, and want you to be top of everybody in school, but you've got to look out for yourself! If you're going to get so baby-hearted and scrupulous about everything, the fellows won't look up to you a minute. Don't you know it? Do you want to fall from where you are now?"

" Who said anything about falling?" said Gilbert, for an answer.

" Well, it amounts to the same thing," said Ray, seriously; " why, Gilbert Starr, you wouldn't have entertained the idea of losing Tom for oarsman, a month ago, no more than you would have planned to assassinate Mr. Winterhalter."

" That's true," said Gilbert, " and I've no idea of losing him now; I was only thinking, and wondering if — well — if — confound it! I wonder whether a fellow can't be good and upright and honorable, without being a baby. That's what I was thinking of."

Ray Hunter did not feel himself competent to answer this question.

"Yes," continued Gilbert, "I wonder if one can't. I wish I knew. I'm sick of some things I do — that we all do."

"Pshaw!" cried Ray, impatiently; "I wish Perry Kent was in Tartary, or somewhere. I know it's all his doings. You're good enough as you are, Gilbert Starr. Come, if you are going to turn into a second edition of that little youngster, I shall go and drown myself."

"Don't trouble yourself, and don't let me hear any more about Perry Kent. He's a good little fellow, though, and it wouldn't hurt us a bit to take pattern of some things. However, I've no intention of doing so, so you may rest in peace, and let me.

Now those chaps have got through their yelling, let's go back to the ash tree. I've got to see Al Turner this minute. Come."

With this, the two crossed over to where the secretary and several of the first class stood.

" Give us your hand, Cap'n Stärr,—give us your hand," said Tom Fowler, stepping out to meet Gilbert; " the battle's o'er, the vict'ry's won, and I'm prodigiously glad of it. Tell you what, boys, I ain't going to get another perfect lesson in six months. If I'd got to study as hard the next month as I have for the last three weeks, you might lay me in the cold, cold grave, and welcome. Not a book will I look at again till Winterhalter compels me to."

" Come, stop your nonsense, Tom," said Gilbert, rather petulantly; " there's business to be attended to. I want the secretary to write a note to Captain Forrest of the River-

side Club, telling him about the prize for the
race, and I want some one to carry it over."

" I'm your man!" cried several.

" All right!—but wait—I haven't got
the permission, yet. Write the note, Al,
and I'll be back in a twinkling;" and
having given this order, Gilbert hurried off
to find Mr. Winterhalter.

He found that gentleman in his study, and
craved the desired permission, which the
Principal granted on condition that the bearer
of the note should be absent from the lawn
but twenty minutes. This was but barely
time enough to perform the errand in, but
Gilbert sent Barry White, who was fleet of
foot, and, from their look-out on the lawn,
the Boat Club saw him paddle across the
river in the little boat which always lay at
the foot of the slope, and from thence hurry
up the steep hill-side path, beyond.

" Now, boys," said Gilbert, after he had

disappeared, " our preparations are all made, and there's nothing to do but wait."

" That's the hardest part of it," said Tom.

" And I want to tell you," continued Captain Starr, " that if we are so unlucky as to lose the pennon that we've worked so hard for, I shall want to hang myself. We *mustn't* lose it. The fellow who fails us to-morrow shall be voted out of the club."

" He'll deserve to be," said Tom, who had no fear for himself.

And, sitting there, they discussed the subject till White returned, and the supper-bell rang; and after supper the lawn was noisy with boys till bed-time, — one and all talking of the event which was to take place on the morrow, and anxiously watching the sky, as its splendor faded, to see whether there was any trace of storm or lowery weather. But the cloudless arch give promise of nothing but a fair day.

# CHAPTER VI.

## THE RACE.

TRUE to the promise of the previous evening, the day dawned fair and splendid.
Never had the sun shone brighter on hill and
river; never did the hill look fairer, or the
river ripple more merrily. The morning
breeze, blowing straight off the cool sea
far below, rustled in the flags which sur-
mounted the school-buildings on both sides
the river, and slowly folded and unfolded
their stars and stripes. And the anxious
eyes which greeted the first flush. of day
could find no charm lacking by which the
morning might be fairer. Yet there was one

drawback, the two clubs thought. Their wish was to have the race in the forenoon, before the heats of the day came on, and while they felt fresh and vigorous for the trial. But this arrangement, Mr. Winterhalter thought, would interfere too seriously with studies and recitations; and Professor Roth was inexorable. So, perforce, they were obliged to wait till afternoon, and then the boys of both schools were to have a half-holiday.

How many times Captain Starr's club visited their boat-house before school-hours, that morning, it would be difficult to tell. There was a constant running to and fro between the lawn and the little white house where the "Triton" lay, — even though all preparations were made, and there was not a thing to do. Gilbert was apparently in the best of spirits, whistling and singing as he made various pilgrimages to the river-edge, and had a word for everybody.

"What a morning 'tis, Perry!" he said, briskly, as he came across the lawn and found his protege by the thorn-hedge; "look sharp, to-day, and you'll see how boats can fly. Get a good place, where you can see it all, and don't let the fellows jostle you out of it. They'll try to do it, but stand your ground and you'll see what a boat-race is. Why, how red and fresh your cheeks are getting! you don't look the same boy as when you came here."

Somehow, Gilbert had begun to take an interest in the boy's welfare; to notice whether he looked ill and pale, or whether he was fresh and bright; which attention, Ray Hunter warned Gilbert, was an awful bad sign; it was making an old grandmother of him, it was spoiling him for play, it would make him the wonder of the whole class; for who ever heard of a big fellow like him looking after such a little chick? However, Gilbert did as he chose.

Was it any wonder that lessons and recitations dragged fearfully that forenoon?—that the boys' minds were somewhere else?—that Tom Fowler, in answer to a question in mathematics, replied, "30 feet long, by 21 inches wide," which happened to be just the dimensions of the "Triton"?—and that Mr. Winterhalter and his assistants secretly thought it had been good policy to have let school out that forenoon? But it came to an end, at last, and they were free.

After a slight lunch, the Boat Club rushed off to their room to dress, and the rest of the school disposed themselves to pass away the time, till they were to be allowed to go to the river-edge, as best they could. At this noon-tide, the sun beat hot and sweltering upon the river, only the faintest breath

of wind stirred in the ash tree and whispered through the water-rushes, and on Riverside there was not the least sign of stir.

"It looks," said Ned Rogers, who still
claimed Perry's attention as much as possible, "as if everybody on Riverside was
dead and buried; but wait till it gets a
little cooler, and you'll see! Them Roth
boys do beat everything to shout and yell.
We've had boat races before, and when their
club beat ours, they made the river ring, I
tell you."

"Do they always beat?" Perry asked.

"*Always?*" said Ned, amazed at such
ignorance; "you'd better guess they don't!
Gilbert beats 'em 'most every time.  Forrest
is their captain, and *he's* smart, but their
crew ain't half so smart as ours, you see.
So they can't come it!"

"Where's the flag?" Perry asked,—"the
prize-flag?"

"Why, don't you know?" said Ned, with another look of pity at such a lack of knowledge; "why, it was carried over to Riverside for their club to see, and then it was put into Mr. Prescott's hands. Mr. Prescott he's umpire, judge, — whatever you call it, — and it's his business to decide who wins, and then to give the flag. Oh, but Mr. Prescott's a nice old fellow! he 'most always makes a speech. Why," continued Ned, "I should think Gilbert would tell you all these things. All the rest of the boys know about them just as soon as they happen. You see, Mr. Prescott ain't partial to either side, so the boys like him first-rate. And he sets the stakes, and times 'em, and does all the business, so that everything is fair and square. But if either — "

Here Master Ned was interrupted in his patronizing explanations by a stir among the boys around them.

"Oh, look!" he cried; "there comes our club, and all dressed. Ain't they grand?" and ran off with the crowd, dragging Perry with him.

Gilbert, with his crew, had just come on to the lawn, and a splendid sight they were in the eyes of the rest of the school. A tumult of applause and exclamations buzzed around them, mingled with the praise and criticisms which are always ready upon boys' tongues. Captain Starr tarried a little while to please the crowd, and very likely not unwilling to hear the words of admiration which his appearance was always pretty sure to call forth, and kept searching the Riverside hill with his gray eyes. But there were yet no signs of stir.

"How confounded hot 'tis!" said Tom Fowler, wiping his forehead; "I shall be as weak as a rag before half-past two."

"It's two, already," said Gilbert, looking

at his watch; "we haven't long to wait. And that makes me think! Who is to be my fag this afternoon? I want to leave my watch with some one, and my pocket-book, too; you know, Ray, I lost 'em both last year. I'm going to look out this time."

There were dozens of applicants for the honor, as it was no ordinary pleasure to be able to say, — among the great crowd on the river-bank, — "*I've* got Captain Starr's watch to keep," or, "Captain Starr put his pocket-book in *my* care," and then to look about on the less fortunate with such an air of supreme exaltation.

Gilbert was puzzled to decide among so many, and just then a sudden thought struck him. "Where's Perry? Perry Kent, come here. You shall be my fag this afternoon, and be sure and be in sight somewhere, if I want you;" and with that he put his treasures into his protege's hands, and thus, unwittingly, made him the object of the envious crowd's persecutions for the whole afternoon. Hardly had the murmurs of dissatisfaction died away when Ray exclaimed, "Look over on Riverside!"

All eyes were turned in that direction. Down the steep path rushed a great crowd of boys, whooping, hallooing, and swinging their hats to their neighbors on Mr. Winterhalter's lawn. Behind them, following at a more sober pace, were the members of the rival Boat Club, distinguished by their blue uniforms.

"Hurrah!" said Tom Fowler; "they're up to time! Give the word, Cap'n, and let us be off."

Gilbert gave the word, and led his men away, — stopping at the little gate in the hedge to say to the crowd which pressed close at their heels, "Now keep good order, and none of your shouting; and don't you let me see any fights on *our* side of the river."

Once off from the lawn, the boys scattered in all directions, — the Boat Club moving in a crimson line straight to their little wharf.

Now the length of river which had been selected as the best for the race was not directly opposite Mr. Winterhalter's; it was a little below. Thither the greater part of the school hurried at once, running and shouting through the low meadows, the fortunate first-comers seizing upon what few shade-trees there were scattered up and down the river-side, and the rest taking their stations all along the bank, wherever they fancied the best view was to be obtained. Perry, with Gilbert's treasures, followed the rest down to the meadows, and found himself a comfortable look-out

under a scraggy willow which no one had
taken possession of, apparently because
it was deemed too far up, or too near the
starting-place. From this seat there was
a long view down the shining pathway of
the river, glowing like molten silver, with
its green bank on either side dotted with
boys, from the willow where Perry sat far
down to the point where something white
glittered and fluttered, marking the end
of the race-course. Here and there, where
the river faded away between the hills, a
lazy sail rounded into view, or, becalmed in
the breathless reaches under the ridge, hung
idle and motionless, not a cloud to shadow
the whole.

Professor Roth's boys had the advantage
of their neighbors, so far as a pleasant look-
out was concerned; for on their side of the
river was the wide, flat road under the hill,
guarded by a railing; and by the railing

were benches where pedestrians might sit and rest under the great shadow of the hill, and here Perry could see them sitting and regarding the whole scene at their ease. Two or three little boats which belonged that side of the river were afloat, and filled with spectators. And there were two or three gentlemen paddling about in a boat, one of whom Perry suspected was Mr. Prescott.

On the top of the ·hill, in the school-grounds, where they could overlook the whole, quite a number of ladies and gentle-men were gathered, and as the time drew nearer and nearer for the race to commence, the number increased.

The blue-coated Riverside Club were the first to come round into their places, and then a great shout went up·from the boys on that side of the river, and the ladies' handkerchiefs waved encouragingly. And when they had taken their place, and their long sharp boat had lain motionless on the water a few seconds, Captain Starr's boat shot out from its mooring, amid the cheers of his friends who were determined not to be outdone in the matter of noise, and glided — a bright crimson line — into position with his rival.

Then there was breathless waiting both sides the river. Perry saw no signal given, heard no word uttered, but suddenly the oars dipped, the boats shot ahead, and the race commenced.

It was a fair sight and pleasant to see, — the long river-view, the crowds on the green banks, the two streaks of red and blue, oars flashing like blades of ruddy gold and dripping sparkling drops, and the sun high and smiling over all. Neither gaining upon the other, straight they steered for the fluttering white signal far down the stream.

A little low murmur of cheers came from the boys on Mr. Winterhalter's side of the river as Gilbert's boat passed, but for the most part the spectators on both sides were quiet and watchful. Some of the little boats, under the shadow of Riverside, dropped down stream to get a better look at the race.

Meanwhile, it was quite as silent in Captain Starr's boat, save some low word of command, and the steady, regular dip of the oars, — the rowers swaying at their task, arms working with a will, eyes on their work, all energies bent for the accomplishment of the feat. Defeat? It was not to be thought of! Shine the sun as hot as it would, arms grow weary, eyes dazzled with the glare, there was only one sight to see, one object to work for, and that the gleaming goal below which grew nearer

every moment. Quietly they came down
to it, turned, and so started homeward.

From Perry's seat under the old willow,
the boats seemed a great distance off, — two
dark lines upon the blue bosom of the river,
— and now his, as well as all eyes, gave anxious heed to their returning. Slowly enough
they seemed to come, as if the heat had told
upon the rowers' arms, and the two boats
were apparently just abreast.

Steadily, steadily onward, gradually growing more distinct, oars beginning to flash
again in the sunlight, drops to sparkle.
How eager and quiet the crowd were! Then
it was, as they began to near, that Gilbert's
boat was found to be a little ahead. Only
a trifle, to be sure; but, perhaps, enough to
win the day, and a great victorious shout
rose up from the boys of Mr. Winterhalter's
school. It came so suddenly, and rang out so
loud and clear, that it almost seemed to have

fallen from the sky.  All was silent as death on Riverside.  On and on they came, straining every nerve, and Gilbert's boat gaining a few inches in every rod.  Perhaps it was Tom Fowler's strokes which told so well just now.  He always seemed to have a good stock of reserved strength for an emergency, and, perhaps, Gilbert would not regret deceiving Mr. Winterhalter after all.

The boys came racing breathlessly up the river-bank, pushing Perry out of his seat, and almost trampling him down in their mad haste to get opposite the goal where the race was to end.  But Perry scrambled to his feet just as the boats shot past the willow tree.

Success seemed certain; the prow of Gilbert's boat was already four or five feet beyond that of the "Mermaid," and the goal but a rod off; his friends were just ready to burst into an exultant shout, when there was a sudden little clash of oars, something checked the speed of both boats, there was a second of wavering, then, with one last great effort, the crew of the "Mermaid" bent all their oars, and shot into the goal—ahead!

Deep silence reigned for a moment on both sides the river. Then shout after shout went up from the Riverside boys,— wild, tumultuous cheers, that were all the wilder and louder because defeat had seemed theirs. And Mr. Winterhalter's boys were silent with dismay and astonishment. What could it mean?

"What *could* have happened to 'em just that moment?— *that* minute of all minutes! Oh, confound it all!" said Rufe Fitch, dancing about in the height of his disappointment; "who ever heard of such a thing? What *could* have happened?"

"Wait and see," said Copp; "there they go, up to Mr. Prescott. Oh, we've lost our flag!"

Gilbert's boat did not go up to the starting-place at all, but turned about and made directly for Mr. Prescott, who was to award the flag. Had they been near enough, his friends would have seen that his face was white with anger; as it was, they heard him say, as his boat floated in front of that gentleman, " Mr. Prescott, they got afoul of us! — they tried to do it all the way up, after we got ahead of them!"

The friends on shore listened eagerly.

" And," added Gilbert, illy concealing his passion, " they're a set of cowards and cheats, the whole of them!"

" Easy, easy, Starr," said Mr. Prescott; " let me inquire into this. Here, Forrest," turning to the captain of the " Mermaid," which had just come alongside, " tell me, on your honor, whether you tried to get afoul of the ' Triton.' "

" On my honor, we did not!" said Forrest, who was as fiery of temper as Gilbert him-

self, and could poorly bear such a suspicion.

"You hear what he says," said Mr. Prescott, turning again to the captain of the
"Triton," "and I think he is right."

"Then he lies!" said Gilbert, fiercely,—
"he lies! and I tell him so to his face!
He tried to get his boat afoul of us for
twenty rods below!"

Two bright red spots burned on either of
Forrest's cheeks, as he said, "I throw the lie
back in his face! I don't know how we got
tangled. I only know that we were pretty
close for a long time, and before I thought,
we struck. I supposed he would strike out
and get in first, for all that; but he didn't,
and so we won."

"Really, Starr," said Mr. Prescott, kindly,
"that is the way I look upon it myself. I
don't think it was intentional, or that Forrest
is capable of such a meanness. So I—"

But Gilbert, perfectly white with passion, had allowed his anger to thoroughly master him. He turned his back upon Mr. Prescott, saying to his men, " Row ashore ; there's no fairness to be got here. Captain Forrest is welcome to the flag, and his own meanness. I won't have anything to do with either !"

So, obdurate to all calls or entreaties, they rowed ashore, where Gilbert would say never a word to the great crowd of boys who gathered around him, but, angry and pale, pushed through them all, and walked slowly up to the house.

9

# CHAPTER VII.

## WHAT A NOTE REVEALED.

THE remainder of the "Triton's" crew stopped at the little wharf. They had enough to do, for a time, with satisfying the volleys of questions which their eager friends poured forth. Ray Hunter told the whole story again and again, always adding what Gilbert had called his rival, and what he had said to Mr. Prescott. By and by Ray went up to the house to find his friend. But the remainder of the crew, and the school-boys, lingered by the river's edge, discussing the event, and were loud in their denunciations of Forrest.

" He's a cheat, anyhow!" said Rufe Fitch,
" and if our Captain's got any spunk, he'll
make him apologize, or fight!"

" You needn't talk about spunk," said
Tom Fowler; " you should have seen Gilbert's face. I declare, if we hadn't been on
the water, I believe the Cap'n would have
pitched into Forrest right on the spot."

" I wish he had," said Sam Copp.

" Water's a plaguy poor place to fight in,"
said Tom, dryly; " and it wouldn't have
looked just right either, before all the ladies
and gentlemen."

" Who cares for that?" said Bob Upham;
" Gilbert's got to look out for the honor
of the school anywhere."

" Don't you worry about the honor," said
Tom; " you never see Gilbert's face look
like that, without something coming of it.
Just wait and see."

" Do you think he'll fight?" queried the

boys, eagerly, — "do you think he'll fight Forrest?"

"If he don't, I will!" said Barry White, "and the rest of his crew into the bargain."

"Pshaw!" said Albert Turner, who was standing apart from the rest and biting his lips with vexation, "let Gilbert manage it. He'll do it best, and suit you all. Come, boys, let's go up and get off these uniforms."

The Boat Club were about to turn away, when there rose a shout from the other side of the river. The Riverside crew had gone ashore with the flag, and their school had received them with cheers and shouts.

"Oh, the cheats!" said Tom, bitterly, as he looked across the river; and the rest of the boys echoed it, and at last the murmur grew into a shout which they flung back across the water,— defiant, menacing. Their rivals answered with a faint cheer, and soon the crowd on the hill broke up, the blue coats disappeared, the boys went up to their grounds, and there was the river as calm and peaceful as ever, beginning to ripple and sparkle with the fresh, late afternoon breeze that was coming up with strong, steady puffs from the sea, which brought the lagging sails into sight.

Meanwhile, Perry had witnessed Gilbert's defeat and seen his anger. He was one of those who gathered about him as he landed upon the wharf, and had tried to restore to him his treasures. But Gilbert gave him no heed, and almost knocked him over as he hurried past without giving him a look. And here he fell again into the hands of the Philistines, who, being in want of an object to vent their wrath upon, took him for that purpose.

Perry, under Gilbert's training, had learned to restrain his tears somewhat, so that the boys failed to make him cry.; but he met with some very rough treatment, and was greatly troubled to keep the watch in his possession, it being his tormentors' object to get it away from him, and pretend to Gilbert that his fag was unfaithful and careless.

Ray Hunter chanced to come down to the wharf just then, to see if the "Triton" had been properly taken care of. Though he was secretly jealous of Perry, and accordingly disliked him, he had the good-hearted-ness to drive the boys away.

"Well," said he, surveying the boy, "you have got a little spirit, I'm glad to see. Now, have you got Gilbert's things safe and sound?"

"Yes," said Perry; "and where can I find him?"

"He's up to the house, and in his room," said Ray soberly; "but I advise you to keep away from him for a while."

" Why?" said Perry, wonderingly.

" Because, he may take your head off; he threw his boot-jack at mine just now;" and then, after laughing a little at Perry's shocked face, added, "You see, Gilbert's got an awful temper, — more than all the rest of us put together, — and when it's up, he's wild as a loon, and don't mind throwing shoes, inkstands, boot-jacks, and things at a fellow's head.    But he'll be better by morning, and you'd better keep away from him till then."

Perry secretly thought that Ray had greatly exaggerated the story, and mentally resolved to see Gilbert at once, and restore his effects before they were wrested from him; so he started for the house, Ray calling to him from the boat-house, —

" If he takes your head off, don't you come complaining to me."

The school had gathered on the lawn,

waiting for the supper-bell to ring, and the Boat Club had removed their uniforms and were there, too, — all but Gilbert, — and as no one offered to molest him, Perry went straight to the room where he knew the Captain must be. The door was shut, and he knocked. No answer came, and there was not a breath of sound within; so he softly pushed open the door. No one in the room but Gilbert, and he sitting on the foot of his bed, with his hands pressed tightly over his face, and his head bowed, as if he were under disgrace; and he did not look up.

Perry hesitated a few seconds, then went up to him, touched his shoulder, and said, softly, —

" Here's your watch and pocket-book, Gilbert; I've kept them safe."

Gilbert turned about, with a face so utterly changed from its usual expression by anger, that Perry instinctively moved back.

"Don't talk to me about watches nor pocket-books!" he exclaimed; "lay them down somewhere, and go away. I won't see anybody."

Perry did as he was commanded, laid them by his side, started to go out the door, and stopped on the threshold. It terrified him to see Gilbert so wild with passion, so lost to all other feelings or sense of good, and while he had not quite the courage to speak again, he longed to stay; and so, betwixt the two impulses, he lingered. Presently Gilbert looked up.

"What! you here?" he cried, getting up; "didn't I tell you to go? Didn't I tell you I wouldn't see any one? Come," grasping his protege by the arm, and dragging him into the hall, "I'll throw you over the balusters!"

Perry made no resistance,—indeed, how could he?—and allowed himself to be dragged along without a struggle, feeling quite confident that Gilbert would come to his senses, and not harm him after all. And he did.

"Well," said he, stopping suddenly short, "I believe I'm possessed with an evil spirit," and put Perry down.

"Oh, Gilbert!" said the little boy, at finding himself thus released.

"There, I suppose I've scared you to death, now," said Gilbert, in a vexed tone; "but look here, little fellow," bending down to him, "I didn't mean it. I forgot myself. You shouldn't have put yourself in my reach. What did you come up here for?"

"To bring your watch and the pocket-book," said his protege, faintly.

"Sure enough; I'd forgotten. Now come back a minute;" and he drew Perry into his room, locking the door behind them. He sat down in a chair by the window, fastening his watch to its chain, and restoring the purse to his pocket.  A little of the great scowl on his forehead was gone, and his eyes were not quite so angry; and Perry, as soon as he could get sufficient resolution, said,—

"Oh, Gilbert! it's an awful thing to be so angry."

Gilbert folded his arms, looked moodily on the floor, and said at last,—

"I've been wronged and insulted, and I've a right to be angry."

To which Perry made no reply, but looked gravely at his friend's face, hoping every moment to see it relent and grow soft.  At last, the corners of Gilbert's mouth began to twitch, and he laughed in spite of himself.

"I declare," said he, "you'd make an owl laugh, if you looked at him with such a face as you have at me for the last ten minutes. What're you thinking about?"

Perry took heart and came up to his protector, saying, in his simple way, —

"Oh, Gilbert, you've been so awful angry!"

"I suppose you're shocked out of your five senses on account of it, too," said Gilbert; "now, I'd no right to scare you to death out in the hall, I acknowledge, but, you see, I can't help it,—being angry, I mean. It rushes all over me at once, and I do all sorts of things before I know it. Now you can't get mad, if you try three weeks."

"But you might *try* not to," suggested his protege, still very earnest.

"There! no more preaching this time," said Gilbert; "I've got other things to think of. You're a good little fellow," putting his arm kindly about Perry, "and it does very well for you to think of these things, and hold your temper, and so on; but for me, — pshaw! it's no use."

"Oh, Gilbert! if you only *would!*" cried Perry, clinging very fast to his arm.

"Well, I *have* thought of it," said his protector, with a slight flush on his face, and making a confession which he would have breathed to no one on earth besides; "but— pshaw! it would be as useless as to try to dip up the river with that inkstand; for, don't you see, I've ten thousand things to pull me down if I undertake? I'm at the head of the school, and there are hundreds of things, not quite right, which I *must* do, and overlook, and call right, — little matters that you never dreamed of, — and I can't do any other way. Why, if I did, I should be pulled down in a twinkling. I must fight for the honor of the school, and keep *that* bright, even if my own does get.— But what's the use of talking? It's all an *impossibility!*

But you may be good and pure, and I love
to see you so; and," he added, quietly, "I
bless the day that ever you came to school.
Now run down to supper, for I heard the
bell ring. Tell them, if they ask, that
I'm not coming. Go!" and Perry had to
obey.

When had Gilbert Starr ever opened his
heart to any one like that? Somehow, after
his protege had gone, he was in no mood
for anger. When his friends of the Club
came up from supper, they found him sitting, with his uniform yet on, by the window, and apparently quite peaceably inclined.
And straightway they went to work at him,
to find whether he was going to fight Forrest, and defend the honor of the school.

This fair day ended with a thunder-storm,
which rose at sunset, and raged half the
night. There were vivid sheets of flame,
sharp crashes of thunder, long, rolling echoes

rumbling in the hills, and wild dashes of rain against the panes. Yet, when morning broke, the sky was blue and cloudless, the earth freshened and all a glitter, and the river rolling and sparkling as merrily as ever.

Perry was up before any of the boys in his room, — the Boat Club were weary with their yesterday's work, — and went out on the lawn while yet it had scarcely an occupant. As he came around the corner of the piazza, he spied a little fragment of white paper, carefully folded, and lying directly in his path. It was muddy, and drenched with the night's rain, and he could not have told what motive prompted him to pick it up. It was likely to prove only a bit of translation, or a solution in mathematics, which some of the first class had thrown away. He strolled on without sufficient curiosity to open the soiled scrap, till he got to the farther end of the lawn, by the hedge-row. Here he pulled

the wet surfaces apart, and found a half-
dozen hurriedly written lines within, — evidently the first thoughts which the writer
had put down towards a note, of which this
was probably the first copy, — for there were
marks of erasion in abundance, and the
whole note wore a look as if the writer had
pondered and hesitated over it. And this
was what he read:

"AT RAINFORD SCHOOL, WEDNESDAY EVENING.

"FORREST, — After what has happened to-
day, you must know that our school expect
you to apologize, or settle the affair in the
only other way it can. be settled. If you
won't apologize, meet me at Rainford bridge
to-morrow night, at sundown. *You know
what for.*        GILBERT STARR."

Perry read the blurred and muddy note
twice through, before he could believe that

he had read aright. He did not quite comprehend the significance of the line in italics, but he was sure the words foreboded some evil. He had heard the boys boasting, the previous afternoon, that Gilbert would teach Forrest a lesson; but what that lesson was to be, he had not imagined. How many ways were there to settle a quarrel? This note hinted there were but two, and if one was apologizing, the other must be — what? Perry was not long in coming to a con- clusion. He had seen enough of the ways of his schoolmates to be pretty certain that the " other way," which was so vaguely hinted of, meant nothing less than fighting. But where had the note come from? Perry walked back to the corner of the piazza and saw that the window above, which opened from Gilbert's room, was raised a few inches. Then it was all plain; it had fluttered down from thence, from off the little

10

writing-desk which always stood before that window, the joint property of the Boat Club.

A crowd of boys came running along the path at that instant, and he was obliged to secrete the note in his pocket, but he went away from them all and sat down, trying to think what it was best to do. You may be sure it seemed a horrible thing to him to imagine Gilbert and the head-boy of Riverside fighting,— fighting for what they deemed honor; and he puzzled his brain with fearful conjectures of the consequences. It was against the rule of both schools, and punishable with loss of rank and scholarship; yet there were few terms passed which did not witness these collisions between the older boys. Generally, Professor Roth and Mr. Winterhalter were ignorant of the affair, and the participators escaped without disgrace or punishment; but occasionally their trespasses

were discovered and the offenders dealt sum-
marily with.

Now what could Perry do? He had not
the least influence to prevail upon the Boat
Club to use efforts in behalf of peace, nor
did he cherish the least hope that Gilbert
would listen to a word from him. And
here was the morning slipping away, and
evening was to bring the fight. Oh, what
could he do? The breakfast-bell rang while
he was pondering, and he was forced to fall
in with the crowd and go to the eating-room.
Gilbert was not there, but came in late,
looking rather dull and tired.

A little buzz of exclamation and whispers
ran around the table as he entered, and
Perry heard Sam Copp say, in a low tone, to
his neighbor, "The Cap'n don't look very
smart for a brush with Forrest."

"No," said Rufe Fitch, in the same tone,

"he looks played out.  I believe I could whip him now, myself."

These remarks were not calculated to put Perry at his ease.  He gave Gilbert many a wistful look from his seat a little way down the long line; but Gilbert looked at no one, and so they failed to accomplish their object. He tried to catch his eye when the boys were leaving the table, feeling sure that Gilbert would stop a minute; but Albert Turner and Ray Hunter hurried him back up to their room, where they stayed till it was almost time for recitations to commence. The first opportunity which Perry had to restore the note was while the bell was ringing for recitations, and Gilbert and some of his class were walking across the lawn toward the hall door.  He ran up to him, tugged at his sleeve, and drew his attention to himself.

"You, Perry?" said Gilbert, with some surprise. "What's wanting?"

For an answer, Perry slipped the note into his hand.

Gilbert opened it, glanced over the contents, and tore it up. "How did you come by this?" he said, sharply.

"I found it under your window, in the path," said his protege; "it was wet and muddy, and had been out all night, I guess."

"Have you shown it to any one?" demanded Gilbert.

"No," said Perry, — "no one."

"Well, I'm much obliged to you," said Gilbert, in a kindlier tone; "it was careless in me to leave it lying about loose, I must confess," and began to move away.

"Oh, Gilbert!" cried Perry; "just wait a min —"

But Gilbert unloosed his hold, with a half-smile on his face which showed plainly he knew what his protege wanted to say, and went in without another word. · Perry looked after him in despair. Would it be best to tell Mr. Winterhalter, and have the affair nipped in the bud? Then Gilbert would be disgraced, and would hate him forever, he thought. Oh, what should he do? There was no one to tell him, no one to ask advice of, and he went into school with a troubled heart. It seemed as if the minutes had never sped so swiftly. Noon came, and Gilbert avoided him. The afternoon session commenced, and still he hit upon no plan, made no decision. And four o'clock came, and school was over. Oh, what to do?

# CHAPTER VIII.

## SKIRMISHING.

THE sun went down behind Riverside in a great cloud of glory. The roofs and steeples stood up warm and splendid in the glow of golden color, and with windows a sparkle, and spires aflame, and long rays of ruddy light striking aslant the river, the picture was brilliant and vivid. Under the shadow of the hill the boatmen cried, and the day's bustle had hardly begun to diminish, but rose in a low, steady hum from where the stevedores were tugging at freights, and unloading the sloops which had come up on the lazy tide.

Perry noted all this sunset splendor, but only with anxious eyes. Supper had been over half an hour, but he was quite confident that Gilbert had not yet gone. At the supper-table he had been as cool and quiet as ever, which was marvellous in Perry's eyes, and after supper he had disappeared with Ray; but such close watch had the little boy kept, that he was sure his friend was yet within the limits of the school-grounds. And he was right, for hardly had the gold color begun to dim before Gilbert and Ray came round the piazza corner, where Perry sat, and arm in arm went down to the hedge gate. There they lingered to whisper and consult for a few minutes, and then Gilbert went down the slope alone, and Ray remained in the gateway, apparently watching his friend, but, as Perry quickly suspected, in reality to prevent any one from following. The little boy gazed at the manly figure till it was hidden by the grassy slope, and then turned away, feeling that if aught was to be done, it must be done quickly. His first impulse was to run to Ray and plead with him to call Gilbert back; but though somewhat excited, he had the sense to remember that it would be the foolishest and most reckless thing he could do, for if Ray once discovered that he was possessed of their secret, he would, in all probability, take him into custody, and thus prevent all interference. This plan being rejected almost as soon as it entered his mind, his next thought was of Mr. Winterhalter. Should he run to his study at once, and disclose the whole? Now in every school-boy's heart there is a certain sense of meanness connected with the thought of disclosing another's plans and actions, even if wrong, or against good rules. Perhaps Perry shared in this. He knew that the fight, and all connected

with it, was wrong, and that Mr. Winterhalter ought to know it; but to reveal the whole,
and bring upon himself Gilbert's indignation
and the persecutions of the whole school,
was naturally more than he felt able to bear.
This plan having been decided against, after
much wavering, another flashed into his head
which seemed so impossible at first that it,
too, was rejected. But the minutes were
flitting fast, and soon it would be too late.
Something must be done quickly, and back
came the project to his head again, this time
wildly urging itself as a last resort. Follow Gilbert? It would cause his protector's
anger, and very likely make him an enemy
forever. Oh, what to do? But there was
just the least faint hope that if he followed
his friend, it would hinder him, and cause
delay; perhaps Gilbert might relent, or
turn back; and with these exceedingly
visionary expectations in his brain, he sud-

denly got up and formed his resolution. He would follow Gilbert.

Now he was not well enough acquainted with the town to know where Rainford bridge spanned the river, and if he found the appointed place of meeting, it must be by keeping Gilbert in sight; and he was out of sight already. Perry left the piazza, and, with a heart beating wildly with excitement and apprehension, prepared to commence his pursuit. Fortunately, Ray, who had watched Gilbert out of sight, now turned away and left the hedge-gate free. But he met Perry face to face, and asked, roughly,—

"Where are you going, Master Kent?"

The boy moved away without answering, and Ray, who fancied his flushed face came from fear of himself, allowed him to pass without molestation, or another thought upon

the subject; and so he went through the
gate and was free to follow.

Oh, how green the grass shone in the
golden light which struck it from the ra-
diant sky, and how the swallows wheeled
over in chippering clouds, dark against the
sky's rich stain! But there was only a
breath to think of it in, and then he was
running, with all his speed, straight to the
river's edge. He gained the little thread of
a path, and paused to look up and down the
wide, wide vista, from where the river rolled
cool under the shadowy hillside, far down
to the waving meadows, where it flashed out
bright and blue as a sapphire. Not a figure
but his own on that side the river. Then
he stopped to consider. The two boarding-
schools, he remembered, were nearly at the
end of Rainford town, and there were few
houses below them; so, in all probability, the
bridge must be further up, toward the centre

of business and travel. Acting upon this thought, he began to run up the narrow path which wound among the rank river-grasses and stunted willows not as high as his head, thinking he should soon overtake Gilbert. But Gilbert had the start, and was no slow walker. On and on the boy ran, giving no heed to the beautiful sights or tender sounds which he passed; seeing not how gay and bright Riverside street, on the opposite bank, had become with promenaders and loungers, who were out to enjoy the fair evening sights and the fresh, steady sea-breeze; failing to see how gayly-dressed boaters were launching their crafts and slowly dropping down stream, with the bright-hued shadows of their costumes trailing in the sea-green water, or, with slowly-plied oars, which threw off glittering drops, worked toward the town. Neither did he hear the echo of their merry laughter, nor their snatch-

es of song, the cry of the late-working stevedores, the lazy wash of ripples on the pebbles, the low sigh of the wind among the
grasses.  All he thought of was Gilbert, —
Gilbert hurrying to fight ! and so pressed on.

Meanwhile, the pursued, little dreaming
of a pursuer, walked rapidly before, and was
as little conscious of the day's dying loveli-
ness as he who came behind.  He walked
briskly, never stopping to look back, and
anxious to meet Forrest according to ap-
pointment.  Now was his a blithe heart, —
cheerful, light, unoppressed?  No; for all
that long walk he was saying to himself as
he hurried along, whisking off the tender
willow sprouts with his idle hands, —

" Gilbert Starr, you're a slave, and the
worst of it is, you've just found it out.
You're going to do what you don't want to
do, what you know is wrong, and what is
against Mr. Winterhalter's rules, just because

you're head-boy of the school, and controlled by that foolish crowd who are always eager for fights and excitement. They say you rule the school, but it isn't so; you're just a poor slave who has to do evil at the bidding of the rest, and that's the plain truth. Oh," sighed he, as he hurried on, " I wish I hadn't found this out! I wish I didn't know what a slave I am,—what a dishonorable, deceitful fellow! Oh, I'm sick of it all!"

Sick of it all, yet without the courage to turn and fight the evil, — to take a bold, manly stand, and declare against what he knew was wrong, and despised as such. This is a kind of cowardice which very bold schoolboys sometimes find themselves affected with, and, because of it, Gilbert Starr was obliged to hurry on to meet his rival.

Meanwhile, Perry had pressed on till Professor Roth's school began to dwindle away into insignificance behind him, and before him the blocks of town-buildings rose up against the sky. He stopped, fearing that in his haste he had failed to discover some by-path which Gilbert might have taken. However, here was the river rippling onward, and no bridge spanning it; so it was plain that the place of destination lay yet beyond. Another rod, and the path took a sharp turn and led up a little ascent toward the thoroughfare of Rainford, and, looking sharply as he turned, Perry spied Gilbert in the act of climbing the fence which shut out the street. Breathless with his long run, he essayed to shout, " *Gilbert!* " but the result was only a faint cry, which failed to reach his friend's ears, and Gilbert passed over the fence and disappeared.

For an instant, Perry stood motionless with disappointment. He had calculated upon overtaking his friend before the town was reached. Gilbert was well used to all the lanes and by-streets, and, if he found himself pursued, could easily pass out of sight and reach of his protege; and, Perry thought, the crowded street was no place to say what he was to say to Gilbert. To turn back, or go forward? that was the question. There was no time for hesitation. He turned and gave one look at the long, shimmering river-vista, weltering in its profusion of sunset dyes, and, after a second of indecision, went on, over the fence, and into Rainford street. There were country-wagons trundling home from market, a great rumble of drays and lumber-wagons, but few people on the sidewalks; so that it was not such a difficult matter to keep Gilbert in view. But if he should happen to look behind! Perry foresaw what would happen, and wisely continued his pursuit from behind the capacious figure of an old gentleman who chanced to be going in the same direction, and screened by this ample protection, made observations at his leisure. Presently Gilbert turned off on another street, which ran at right angles with the first, and here Perry was obliged to follow at his peril, for the old gentleman kept straight on, and there was nothing to shield him from Gilbert's eyes, should he chance to look around. But Captain Starr had other thoughts upon his mind, and not the faintest possible suspicion of a pursuer; and so, in a short time, they came out where there was a great reach of crimson sky beyond, where, again, there was a glimpse of the river and a sound of its ripples against stone piers. Here was Rainford bridge, and there, leaning idly over the rail to look into the water, was a figure which Gilbert walked up to without delay, and touched upon the shoulder. When it turned, Perry saw that it was Forrest. Now

MEETING OF THE RIVAL CAPTAINS.  Page 162.

he could go no nearer without being seen, and not daring to accost Gilbert then, he hid himself behind a tree-trunk, in anxious waiting for what was to follow. The rival captains conversed a few minutes, and then came to the end of the bridge, went over the side of the abutment, and disappeared. Had they jumped into the river? Perry wondered. Where *had* they gone? He followed cautiously, and peeped over. Instead of waves and ripples, he saw that the abutment rested upon a grassy slope, — the brink of the river. From this sprang the curve of the stone arch, and under its shade and secrecy the head-boys had gone to fight for *honor*.

As he leaned over, Perry could hear the faint sound of their voices, and in an agony of apprehension looked about him for some means of descending. The rivals had evidently gone down on the projecting cor-

ners of stone-work; but Perry hardly had
the strength and nerve for such an under-
taking. It was a rough place for a fall, and
there were scattered bits of rock at the base;
so that he now seemed as far from the accomplishment of his object as ever. He
leaned far over, waiting, anxious, listening
fearfully for the sound of blows. People
came over on the bridge, and as they passed
wondered what that little red-faced, tired-
looking boy was listening to; and one motherly old lady, coming home from a tea-party,
with work-bag and umbrella, threw up her
hands in alarm, and cautioned him against
losing his balance and breaking his neck.
There was such a long silence of the two
voices, and the river grated so noisily on its
pebbles, that Perry could bear the suspense
no longer. He waited till there was no one
coming across the bridge, then clambered
over the abutment. Clinging to the jagged

edge with both hands, stepping from fragment to fragment, bumping his chin, scratch-
ing his face, tearing his jacket, and, toward
the last, making a misstep and falling heavily, he got to the ground at last, almost
breathless. Then, without waiting to consider, or to think of the consequences, he ran
under the arch, saw blows dealt by each,
and, without waiting to see more, threw
himself upon Gilbert, clinging to him with
all his strength.

"Perry Kent!" cried Gilbert, almost pet-
rified with astonishment, and could hardly
believe his eyes.

"Oh—stop—stop, Gilbert!" was all the
breathless boy could utter.

Of course the combatants ceased hostilities, being, each of them, startled into an
armistice by this sudden apparition. Gilbert was the first to find his tongue.

"Where on earth did you drop from?"

he said, looking at Perry, and then up at the great arch above them, as if he expected to see the hole where he had fallen through.

"I followed you; I knew you were going to — to — fight," gasped Perry, "and — and I thought — Oh, Gilbert!" and here he came very near bursting into tears.

Gilbert was touched. Why had this little fellow followed him such a long, long distance, risking his neck and limbs and almost his life, to prevent him from fighting? Did he deserve such devotion? So it happened that he was quite disarmed of the harsh words which it was his first impulse to shower upon his protege's head, but said, reproachfully, —

"Now, Perry, you're too bad to trouble me in this way. Don't you see, you've almost killed yourself with running, and you'll be sick for it, and then the whole affair will have to come out?  Did you mean to get me disgraced?"

Perry's only answer was a tighter clasp about his protector.

Gilbert was silent, biting his lips with anger at the interruption, yet puzzled and softened by the proof of such love and attachment.  He looked up at his opponent.

Forrest had looked on with astonishment at first, then with a scornful face ; but now, as their eyes met, he was regarding Gilbert with a look which seemed to say, " I wonder if you're the same Gilbert Starr who was trying to batter my face a few minutes ago?"

Gilbert looked down, and tried to make himself angry again, and rouse his passion sufficiently to cast Perry off and fight for the honor of his school.  But he made but poor work of it.  He did not feel particularly vengeful toward any one, and the honor of the school seemed a somewhat confused and misty excuse for a fight, just then; and he even debated within himself whether it were not a possible matter to stand up, at once, and come out against the whole round of practices which he was beginning so to hate.

What good resolve he might have made in this softened mood was suddenly dashed to pieces by Forrest, who picked up his hat from off the grass, saying, with a curl of his lips, "I suppose I may consider myself at liberty to leave, now. The honor of Rainford school is vindicated, I presume. Your prowess —"

Gilbert slowly straightened himself up, whispering to Perry, "Let go of me, little chap, and run home. I've got to fight. Run home, I say, — there's a good fellow."

But Perry had no intention of releasing his hold so long as there was the least hope of stopping hostilities, and replied, "Oh, don't mind what he says, Gilbert! Let him go, and don't listen, and oh, Gilbert, come home with me!"

"Yes, better go home with him," said Forrest, lightly; "I advise you to."

Gilbert's eyes flashed, and he stood up tall and straight, with his protege clinging to him, saying, "*You* won't go home yet, Forrest."

"All right," said his rival, tossing his hat back upon the grass, "I'm at your service," and stood there, looking cool and impudent.

"Oh, do, *do* come home, Gilbert!" Perry begged; "let him call you a coward or any-thing,—it ain't worth minding. It's more cowardly to stay and fight."

Gilbert believed him in his secret heart, but said, "I'm not going home yet, but you shall go, Perry. I tell you you *must!* Don't you say another word, but go straight home and stay there. If you refuse, I'll

never forgive you nor speak to you again.
Why, child, you never saw a fight in your
life! Go home, go home!—Perry Kent,
*go home!*" Gilbert was in earnest.

Perry turned away with a smothered sob.
He never distinctly remembered climbing
the steep abutment, nor the run through
Rainford streets, nor anything, in fact, till
he found himself once more in the river
meadows, where all the golden color had
faded into sombre gray; where the sobbing
of the river in the grass was mournful, the
chirping swallows gone, the wind sighing
heavily, and great fireflies flashing across
his path, waving, sailing, rising high over
his head, and when he was once there, running toward home as if for dear life. He
was not at all undecided, now, what to do.

# CHAPTER IX.

### WHO VANQUISHED THE FOES.

A LITTLE later, the door of Mr. Winterhalter's study flew open, and in
rushed a breathless figure. It burst in upon
them so suddenly, and with so little warning, that the worthy couple who were sitting
there started to their feet in surprise, Mrs.
Winterhalter upsetting her work-basket, and
sending a shower of spools over the floor.

"Now!—who?—what—why, it's Perry
Kent, Mr. Winterhalter!" she exclaimed,
throwing up her hands to emphasize her
astonishment. "Now something's happened,
I'll warrant. Do you see, he's out of

breath and ready to drop down? Why, my little fellow," going up to Perry, and putting her motherly arms about him, " have those naughty boys been tormenting you again?"

"Yes," said Mr. Winterhalter, leaving his papers, "what's happened, my little fellow?"

"Oh," cried Perry, as soon as he could get breath enough for the purpose, " Gilbert is — is fighting — Forrest!"

"Gilbert Starr?" said Mr. Winterhalter, looking incredulous.

"Yes — Gilbert — Forrest!" gasped Perry, with his second breath.

"Gilbert Forrest?" said Mrs. Winterhalter, who was somewhat excited; "why, there's no such boy in —"

"Gilbert *and* Forrest, my dear," said the Principal, who began to comprehend the whole. " Now tell me where they are, Perry, and bring me my hat, if you please, Mrs. Winterhalter."

Perry made out to tell Mr. Winterhalter where the combatants were secreted, and then that gentleman hurried away, leaving the boy in his study. Mrs. Winterhalter put him into the easy-chair, which her husband had just vacated, and went about looking for her spools, taking sly looks at Perry's face meanwhile. When she had restored her treasures to their former orderly condition, and taken up her basket of mending, she exclaimed, —

"Dear me, what trouble boys *do* make! Likely enough Mr. Winterhalter will take his death of cold, going off to that damp river.  And Gilbert Starr, just think! — our head-boy fighting with the Professor's, when it's against all the rules.  Dear, dear! I don't know, I'm sure I don't know what Gilbert can be thinking of."

She took a quiet observation of Perry's face, and decided that it would not do to ask him any questions yet, and so continued her soliloquy, the motherliness in her heart brimming over into a smile upon her kind face as she said, "Boys will be boys, always, I suppose, and they aren't half so bad as they pretend; but for our Gilbert to go off to that old bridge to fight, really, it— I don't know what Mr. Winterhalter will do to him. He's so—"

"Oh!" Perry interrupted, anxiously, "do you think — will — will he punish Gilbert?"

"There, there, don't worry," said the good lady, kindly; " I didn't say he'd punish Gilbert. I don't know anything about it, you know. Mr. Winterhalter is dreadful set against fighting, as he ought to be, I think, and Gilbert sets an example for the rest. Now, dear, perhaps you won't mind telling me how you came to find out about the affair."

Perry revealed the whole, encouraged, whenever he faltered, by the good lady's kind tones; and before he could quite finish, down went needles and mending, and Mrs. Winterhalter got up.

"You poor, tired-out child!" said she, coming up to Perry, and smoothing back his hair; "you've run clear to Rainford bridge and back, to-night! And here, if I can believe my eyes, your chin is scratched and bleeding, and your hands — fie! I really don't believe Gilbert Starr deserves so much. Well, I don't wonder you're out of breath, poor boy. Here, let me look at your face, dear;" and with that, Perry had to undergo all sorts of soothing care, which was not ungrateful in his wearied state. "There!" when she had done, "now don't you worry another bit. Mr. Winterhalter will separate them, I'll warrant; and besides, it's getting too dark to fight. If Gilbert persists in being such a naughty boy, I shall have to talk to him myself. Why, dear, it's a shame that he didn't bring you home after such a long chase! But that's the way with boys, they don't think: if they did, they would be different creatures many a time. Mr. Winterhalter has had hundreds of boys here, in his day, and there were but precious few of them that I couldn't find something to love in,"—Perry could well believe that,—"and when I see a smart, noble fellow like Gilbert, that has almost as much to do with governing the boys as Mr. Winterhalter himself, I think,—well, it's not much wonder if he does get astray, and self-ish, perhaps, with so many to honor and praise him. But wait a while and you'll see. If there's the right material in him, God helping, he'll make a man to look up to.

Now, dear, I won't tire you to death with my long talk, but let me ask one more question. Did Gilbert drive you away?"

Perry's grieved face was a sufficient answer, and the good lady said, cheerily and briskly, —

" There, I suspected it all the time. Now don't worry; he'll like you as well as ever to-morrow morning; I promise you he shall. And now, hadn't you better go to bed, dear? There's no telling when Mr. Winterhalter will get back; and you're so tired that you're head droops. Come with me and have a glass of milk, and then go up to your room. It's almost time for the last bell to ring."

The last bell did ring while they were in Mrs. Winterhalter's parlor, and Perry heard the rush of feet up the stairs, and after having his glass of milk, started to go too. The kind lady bent over and kissed him, as she bade him good-night, and he had to hurry away as fast as possible to hide his tears, — the kiss was so like mamma's, — she calling after him, —

" Go straight to sleep, and not lie awake to think of what has happened."

When Perry got up-stairs, he found all the first class there, — of course excepting Gilbert, — they having just come in.

" Hello ! here's the little lamb," said Tom Fowler, as he entered; " why, what late hours you keep, little lambkin ! 'Pears to me you're getting worse and worse. We must institute a committee of investigation straight off. Can't allow such irregularities, — no, sir ! — it's against our principles."

 Perry was accustomed to this railing, in Gilbert's absence, and having other thoughts to fill his mind, paid very little attention to it.

Tom made a few more remarks, at which

his fellows laughed, and then left Perry in peace, Ray Hunter having said to him, —

"Take care, Fowler, and not hit too hard; you know I consider Gilbert's affairs the same as mine, when he's away;" and Gilbert's name being mentioned, the whole class fell to talking about him.

The little boy took off his clothes, and knelt down in the shadow of his corner to pray. It seemed to him the words had never crowded so fast to his lips before, nor in -his heart, with such longing for God's pity and help, such hope that he would soften Gilbert's heart and make it an humble one, such yearning for the dear friend whom he had estranged. He laid his head upon the pillow, sighing heavily, and almost ready to cry when he thought of Gilbert as an enemy. He was quite confident that he would never forgive him for exposing the fight to Mr. Winterhalter, and with him for an en-

emy, and the rest such persecutors, what
would school be?  True, Mrs. Winterhalter
had promised that Gilbert should like him
as well as ever;  but how was it possible for
her to compass that?   Perhaps the little boy
had never known how much he loved and
leaned upon his protector, or to what a great
extent he had depended upon him for happiness;  and now that this friend was to be an
enemy, the sudden change brought back the
same loneliness which he had experienced
when he came to Rainford with a fresh grief
in his heart.   He almost repented having
told Mr. Winterhalter; then he resolved that
it was right, and he would be glad; then,
again, he was plunged into the depths of
sorrow, and wept with his face in the pillow.
By and by he remembered Mrs. Winterhalter's injunction to " go straight to sleep,"
and tried to follow it;  but this he found to
be of no use, and so composed himself to

wait Gilbert's appearance with a trembling heart. And just here he became conscious of what Albert Turner and the rest were talking about.

"It looks rather strange," the secretary of the Boat Club had said, "that Gilbert should have held back so about fighting. Why, I've known him fight just because one of Roth's boys chose to call our school a set of 'grannies,' and you'll all allow that it was nothing, compared with the insult Forrest gave us."

"He was anxious enough to fight at first," said Bob Upham; "but he cooled down wonderfully sudden. What the reason was I don't pretend to know."

"He isn't the same fellow he used to be," said Barry White, decisively,—"not half the spirit in him, I think!"

"I wouldn't be surprised to see some one

else in his place as head-boy, captain, and all that," said Tom Fowler.

Gilbert's friend, Ray, could bear it no longer. "Oh, shame on you all!" he cried out; "Tom Fowler, you're a traitor to your Captain! Barry White, Gilbert's got more spirit in one of his eyelashes than you've got in your whole body, and as for Bob, his opinions never hurt a mosquito that I heard of. Now I know Gilbert as well as any of you, and I say he's just as much fit to be head-boy and rule us all as ever he was! To be sure, he *did* hold back from the fight, and he wouldn't tell his reasons, but you'd all of you make a pretty fuss, I guess, if you couldn't have your private opinions without being blamed for it. You know you would! and if I were Gilbert, I'd stick to 'em till death for no other reason."

"Whew!" said Tom, "Ray is a perfect

spitfire. Go in, my dear, I like to hear you."

" I sha'n't 'go in,'" said Ray, "for Gilbert don't need it. He's able to fight his own battles; but I won't hear him talked against behind his back. No more would you, if he were your friend."

" He *is* my friend, I guess," said Tom; " I'd like to see the fellow that would dare say he wasn't."

" Of course," said Bob Upham, " we all acknowledge him for a leader, and a friend, too, as for that matter."

And ere long they all had avowed pretty much the same thing. Perry listened to this wrangling among the Boat Club, and rejoiced to hear that Gilbert had been averse to the fight. He was pretty sure that there would have been no fight at all, could his friend have had the courage to have stood out against the importunities of his friends.

These disputes between members of the Club were no rare occurrence. Indeed, it seemed to be as Tom Fowler said, " the more they quarrelled, the better they liked each other," and the wranglers seldom got farther than words. Now, one by one, they had got into bed, and the room grew silent, save a word now and then which showed they were all awake, and apparently waiting some one's return. They little imagined that the boy in the corner knew who it was, or that he waited for the sound of footsteps on the stairs quite as eagerly as the rest of them. The windows were open, and the night-breeze came in, flaring the lamp-flame and causing it to shoot grotesque shadows over the ceiling and wall, and such a silence had fallen over the house that it almost seemed as if the river's low ripple could be heard.

About this time two figures came up the

lawn from the river. They were Mr. Winterhalter and Gilbert Starr. They were talking in low tones as they came into the school-grounds, — the Principal very earnestly, Gilbert quite in his usual voice. They went in at the front-door, under the piazza, and into the brightly-lighted study. Mrs. Winterhalter looked up with a pleasant smile, and placed a chair for Gilbert.

"Some milk, if you please," said the Principal, in his usual kind tone; " we've had a long walk, and Gilbert must be even more thirsty than myself. Stop!" as his wife rose, " I'll go and get it myself, and we'll have it here by ourselves in the study. . Sit down, sit down, Gilbert; I'll be back presently."

Not a word of reproach in his tone; it seemed even more genial and friendly than usual. So Gilbert was fain to sit down in the easy-chair by Mrs. Winterhalter's basket of mending, and that good lady passed away the time very pleasantly till her husband came back with the milk-pitcher and tumblers. She made Gilbert drink of the beverage till he could drink no more, made no allusion to his transgression, save by anxiously inquiring if he were hurt, and then asked him to stay to prayers. This last request startled him a little, but he acquiesced, and, for the first time in his life, heard a prayer offered directly for himself. It was not such a prayer as the Pharisee made, thanking God that he was not as other men, but tender and hopeful, asking God to give their head-boy strength and grace to walk uprightly, a pure heart, that he might love the Right, a good influence, that his rule might shelter no evil and forward no wrong. Then they let him go, with a kind good-night, Mrs. Winterhalter following him into the hall to whisper, " Gilbert, there's a little boy up-stairs whom a kind word would make wonderfully happy."

The first class heard steps on the stairs, and immediately every head in the room was raised, save Perry's, and as many pairs of eyes were bent upon the door. Gilbert came in, — smiling, when he found them all looking at him.

" Well ! " came impatiently from Tom Fowler's lips.

" Don't keep us a minute in suspense ! " cried White; while Ray exclaimed, " Oh, Gilbert ! he hasn't whipped you ? "

" No," said Gilbert, coolly, sitting down to take off his shoes, " neither of us whipped the other.  Mr. Winterhalter interfered."

Perry's heart, you may be sure, was making wild beats all this time.  A low cry of dismay went from lip to lip at this disclosure.  No one had imagined such a turn of affairs.

"Winterhalter interfered?" cried Tom, who was the first to recover his speech; "why, how could that be? Not a soul but those in this room knew of the affair!"

"There's a traitor somewhere," said Ray, fiercely, "and I'd just like to find him!"

At this all the Boat Club swore upon their honor that they were not the guilty party.

"But," demanded Ray, "who else can it be? No one out of the Club knew that a meeting had been appointed, or a time set. It *must* be one of us! Who *could* it have been, Gilbert?"

At this juncture Perry held his breath, expecting to hear his name disclosed, and bitterly denounced. He knew that, if it were, he might expect little peace that night.

"Well," said Gilbert, "it's too late to talk of the traitor now. The affair is all over. Mr. Winterhalter came in upon us, and stepped between, and Forrest and I had to shake hands and promise peace on our honor. So we're under bonds, you see. And Ray, old fellow, don't ask any more questions to-night, for I'm too tired to answer."

"Wait,—just one more," said Tom. "Is Winterhalter awfully stirred up about it?"

"Yes, are you going to be suspended?" said Albert Turner.

"Pshaw!" interrupted Ray, "of course he isn't. If he has to leave school, I'll go too!"

"Let him answer our question," grumbled Tom.

"Well," said Gilbert, "Mr. Winterhalter and I had a talk, coming home, and he said J was not to be punished. That's all I know about it; so go to sleep, the whole of you!"

Perry drew a sigh of relief, and said to

himself, " He's too big-hearted to tell them about *me* and let them torment me; but oh! I know he'll never speak to me as long as he lives."

Pretty soon the lamp was extinguished, and the boys began to breathe heavily in slumber. Perry, with a heavy heart, was about to turn his face toward the wall and obey Mrs. Winterhalter's injunction at last, when a soft stir beside his bed caught his attention. Then, close beside his face, a dear voice whispered, " Perry, are you asleep?"

" Oh, Gilbert!" the boy almost cried aloud, and put out his hands and found the speaker's own.

" Hush!" said the voice, " or the rest will hear. Now — I thought that — that perhaps you would think me angry with you, after what had hap —"

" I did, I did!" interrupted the boy's

voice, tremblingly, "and, oh, Gilbert, aren't you?"

" Not the least, you foolish little fellow. I don't like tell-tales, but—I like you. Now go to sleep, and forget what has happened. But wait and tell me, you queer little chick, what you took such a race and such a risk for to-night? Why, if the boys knew, they would almost tear you to pieces."

" It was — for *you.*"

There was a long silence in which Gilbert held the little boy's hands in his, or rather let them lie where they had placed themselves, and then he turned away without another word, save a soft " Good-night." And, to quote Mrs. Winterhalter, a little boy went to sleep " wonderfully happy."

# CHAPTER X.



TO everybody's surprise, Gilbert Starr was not punished. Neither did Mr. Winterhalter seem to take any notice of the occurrence, and this was the greatest mystery of all. Only Gilbert knew what had passed between them on their homeward walk, and he revealed nothing.

It took but a few hours for the news of the occurrence to reach every ear in school, and then there was a great commotion.

Captain Starr rose at once in the estimation of his followers, and was never so popular as now; but the question on every lip was, "Who could the traitor be?"

"Only let us get hold of him!" said Sam Copp; "we'll teach the villain to inter-fere with our business!" and this was the sentiment of the whole school. The lower classes, of which Rufe Fitch headed one and Copp the other, laid the charge of treason at the door of the first class, and the Boat Club, angered at the suspicion, yet unable to refute it, secretly set Ray Hunter to investigating the matter. As yet, no one suspected Perry Kent. The improbability of his being connected with any such affair, prevented the least suspicion from attaching to him. Why, even shrewd Rufe Fitch would have sooner brought the charge against any other boy in school than against "that baby-faced thing," as he termed Captain Starr's protege, — such a charge would have been so utterly ridiculous in everybody's eyes.

It would almost seem that Gilbert Starr

13

might now have the courage and resolution to make a stand against the evil which he wished to combat. Mr. Winterhalter's leniency reproached him, — *how much*, he would have revealed to no one, — and the memory of his prayer haunted him. But, to counteract these good influences, there was Gilbert's high, strong pride, which was gratified by his rule and sway over the school; and how could he endure to lose it? — for lose it he must, the instant he dared to oppose any habit or caprice of his followers. And there was Ray Hunter, who had more influence over him than any boy in school, hardly excepting Perry Kent, and this friend of the Captain used all his influence to keep him in the same old paths, protesting, entreating, if Gilbert swerved but a hair's-breadth from old practices.

And so day after day went by, and found him yet countenancing those things which his heart rebelled against, because he had not the courage to lose his high position and take an humbler one; because his friends would desert him, and he could not bear the thought of such a loss; because he knew that the whole school would sit in judgment and declare him a weak, unmanly, soft-hearted fellow for wanting to be a better one, and such a brand was more than he could or would bear. If he could not be better without being unmanly, he would rather keep in his old ways, he thought; and whether manliness and goodness could be united, was a perplexing question in his heart. The school, to all appearances, had decided not. Was he strong enough to go against them all? — to prove their mistake by his own conduct? To commence and miserably fail, — that would be shame and anguish, and ruin to the cause! — and so he waited, and pondered in doubt and per-

plexity, deciding for neither the right nor
the wrong.   Could *you* have done better?

Now Gilbert kept all these thoughts to
himself, and observing Ray Hunter did not
dream of their presence.   He sometimes
saw that his friend was silent and thoughtful, where he had once been gay and boisterous, but he did not guess the truth, nor
imagine Gilbert's thoughtfulness to result
from anything but ordinary school-events.
He took great heart when he saw the Captain rise to the height of popularity again,
and assert his authority as of old ; and thinking to do his friend a great service, he re-
doubled his exertions to discover who had
betrayed the combatants into Mr. Winterhalter's hands.   In the first place, he took pains
to ascertain who was out latest on that evening.   It proved to be Perry Kent ; but Ray
thought little of that till he discovered that
the same boy had been seen to go out the

hedge-gate, a little after sun-down, and then
he remembered meeting him himself, and how
Perry's face flushed as their eyes met.  Then,
coupling this with the fact that the boy did
not come to his room till nearly an hour
after his usual bed-time, and with the fact
that Gilbert himself had all along been
strangely silent upon the important question of "Who was the traitor?" his suspicions suddenly deepened into certainty,
and he was confident that he had discovered
the delinquent.

"He must have overheard us talking about
the fight when we thought him asleep!"
he thought, indignantly; "and Gilbert has
known it all the time!" Ray was amazed
and indignant and sorry at the same time,
— amazed that the traitor should prove to be
Perry Kent, the last boy to be suspected, —
indignant that he should disclose their secrets
to Mr. Winterhalter, and because Gilbert

had hidden the truth from himself, — sorry, because Gilbert, in his opinion, had fallen below his dignity by deigning to " hide that little baby-faced, tale-telling, *mean* rascal from the punishment he deserves !"

The more Ray thought of it, the angrier he grew. His first impulse was to spread the news of his discovery all over the school, and let Perry Kent suffer the consequences. Very likely he would have done so, had he not chanced to remember that such a disclosure would bring reproach upon Gilbert as well as the traitor; so he desisted for the present, and went in search of the Captain at once.

It was the time between the close of school and tea, and Gilbert chanced to be the only one in the room, when Ray came up-stairs, and as he was busy over some lessons, he did not turn his head at the sound of his friend's well-known steps. When he did look up, wondering at Ray's silence, it was to see that young gentleman standing by his table, and looking down upon him with eyes that were very angry, if not disdainful.

Gilbert waited for Ray to explain himself; Ray waited for Gilbert to speak. At last, " Well, what's the matter?" came from Gilbert. " What have I done this time?"

" Something which would be called meanness in any one else," said Ray, indignantly; " you've deceived me and the whole school at once!"

Gilbert's face flushed a little as he answered, —

" You can't be beat for saying hard things, Ray Hunter. Now explain, for I don't understand."

" You might, if you'd think. I've just discovered who the traitor was that gave our secret to Mr. Winterhalter."

"Was it I?" smiled Gilbert.

"Of course not; you aren't capable of *that*; but you've hid the one that *did* do it from the whole of us,—from me, that you've no right to deceive; from your Club, that has as much right as yourself to know the offender. I declare, I've a good mind to tell the whole school at once!"

Gilbert took no notice of this half-threat, but coolly asked,—

"How did you find out?"

"Oh, by putting this and that together. It's all as plain as day to me, now. That rascal, Kent, listened and overheard our plan, then kept"—

"Excuse me," said Gilbert; "but that little rascal did no such thing. If you must know, he found the copy of the challenge, which I sent Forrest, under my window. That's how the secret came out.

He said nothing to any one, but gave it back to me."

Ray was surprised, but not mollified.

"So he was dishonorable enough to tell of what came into his hands by chance! But why didn't you forbid him to breathe a word of it to any one? Why didn't you give him a good thrashing when you found out what was done? Why didn't you let us all know?"

"Because," said Gilbert, "it would have been like throwing him into a den of lions; you'd have tormented him to death! Now the little fellow ran the risk of your revenge, and mine, too, and came clear up to Rainford bridge to stop the fight, and all for my sake, because he thought it was wrong, and I was making a brute of myself. That's more than *you* or the Club ever did for me; and since he stood by me and ran such risk, now I'll stand by

him, and keep you and the whole school
off, if I die for it!"

Ray fell back in astonishment. At last
he said, "But, Gilbert, just think of the
consequences! They'll say you're a coward,
and bribed Kent to tell Winterhalter. Don't
you see?—they'll claim that, and say you
shelter him to pay for it."

But Gilbert's spirit was roused. "Consequences!" he exclaimed; "I don't care
for the consequences! I'm able to shelter
this little fellow from you all, and I'll do
it! I should be a brute and a coward if I
didn't."

Ray knew his friend too well to think
it would be of any further use to oppose
him. So he changed his tactics, and was
gentle and persuasive. He drew a chair up
to Gilbert's table and sat down, saying,
"Now I haven't told any one of this, but
I've got to, you see, for the Club set me

to find out. Now there's no need of men-
tioning your name, if you'll only give up
this confounded Perry. If he tattles, let
him take the consequences, but don't you
be dragged down with him! Oh, Gilbert,
just listen to reason, and let him take care
of himself."

Gilbert's gray eyes flashed as angrily as
Ray's had done, and he got up from his
chair, saying, "I sha'n't listen to this any
longer. If you aren't trying to drag me
down, who is?"

Ray saw he had gone too far, and repented. He pulled the Captain back, saying, "There, forgive me!—don't mind
what I said. Come back here a minute.
Now what shall I tell the Club when I
report?"

" Whatever you like," said Gilbert coldly ;
" it will make no difference with me."

" But, old fellow," putting his arm about

the Captain, " you're offended with me now.
Don't you know I wouldn't do a thing to
harm you an atom, and that's why I've got
myself into ill-favor, — by trying to do this
thing for your sake?"

" That's true," said Gilbert, reflectively,
and gave his friend his hand.

" Now," said Ray, as he grasped it, " forgive me, and I'll tell the Boat Club a fib.
They shall never know any —"

But Gilbert snatched away his hand, saying, " Look here, Ray! don't you see what
we've come to?  We've got so that we don't
mind a fib, or deceit, or a plain lie now and
then, if it works for our interest.  Our
honor is all a sham.  We do something *dishonorable* every day of our lives, and think
nothing of it!  Why, don't you see what
*shams* we are? Are your eyes blinded? Don't
you feel it in your heart?  Oh, I'm sick of
it all!  I hate it!  I loathe myself!  Tell

the Club if you like, Ray, and I'll make a stand for the right. It's got to come sometime, and it might as well come now. I'm sick of this kind of life, and I want to be a better fellow, and I've got to make a commencement; and if I'm to be pulled down, I can bear it as well now as any time."

Ray's arm slid off his friend's shoulder, and he moved backward. His astonishment was written upon his face. He plainly did not know what to say or think.

As for Gilbert, he looked at his friend, hoping for some word of encouragement. Now that this confession was made to his nearest friend, it did not seem so hard to stand out before the rest, and allow them to read his intentions. He would now care nothing for the school's sneers, but go bravely on and show them that —

Just here there came an interruption in the shape of Barry White, — an interruption which was destined to dash all Gilbert's hopes and resolutions in pieces, and, strangely enough, at the very moment when he had resolved to bravely carry them out.

So, ofttimes, our best, our purest motives are frustrated by some evil which suddenly thrusts itself upon us, overshadowing and driving them away, and leaving us forlorn and guideless, knowing not which way to turn. But if we have the heart and patience to wait and trust on, a kind Hand presently rends the darkness and leads us up and out into day.

Barry White came in, saying, "Ah, Captain, you're the very fellow I want to see! Do — why, you here, Ray? — you see, Cap, the queerest thing has happened, and you're the one to tell me what to do. Listen a minute, please."

"Certainly," said Gilbert, turning about

to listen, though he was secretly annoyed by this interruption.

" Well," said Barry, " it's all about my gold pencil. You see, I didn't want it this morning, when I dressed, so I left it out there on my table. When I came to get it this noon, it was gone. I've been ask-ing all the fellows, since school, and they remember seeing it there."

" So it's gone?" said Gilbert, vaguely, still thinking of something else.

" Yes, and that's what's so funny. Of course our fellows can't steal, and the other classes never come in here. What can I do, Captain?"

Gilbert got up and walked to the table, looked among the papers, and saw it was not there. He came back, saying, " Sure it isn't in some of your pockets?"

Barry turned his pockets wrong side out.

"Are you sure you laid it there?" said Gilbert, looking puzzled.

"I *know* I did; Turner will tell you so, so will Tom, — they saw it there."

"So did I," said Ray.

"That is curious," said Captain Starr. "Haven't you any idea about it, — no suspicions, White?"

·Barry shifted uneasily in his chair, looked at Ray, then at the Captain, and said at last, "Why, if — if our fellows are above suspicion, and you'll allow they are, and none of the other classes can come in except Perry Kent, I can't help but think that — that —"

Here Barry hesitated and looked at Gilbert, not knowing how far he might venture in his suspicion.

Gilbert's face had grown suddenly white, but he said, "Go on!" and White finished with, "I can't help but think it was he,

you see, because there's no one else to suspect."

Ray Hunter, though he disliked Perry
Kent, felt sorry for Gilbert then, and was
fain to offer a word of consolation.

"Pshaw, White!" he exclaimed, "likely
enough the fellows have hid it away for a
joke. You'd better be certain before you
accuse."

"Yes," said Gilbert, "but we *will* be
certain. This is something which concerns
me. Ray, send all our class up here."

Ray went off to do as he was ordered,
and Gilbert shut up his books, thinking it
was a very unfortunate moment for such
disagreeable business to befall him. Very
likely it was only one of Tom Fowler's
jokes, but if it should *not* be, and the pencil
was really stolen, and it should be proved
that no one but Perry Kent had — Gilbert
would allow himself to think of no such

14

possibility, and walked away to the window. There he saw his protege playing on the lawn below.

" Oh !" he thought, " if I do find that I'm deceived in him, that he isn't the good, warm-hearted—but pshaw! I. won't think of it! He can't be anything else."

Ray was not long in finding all the inmates of the first room, and taking them up-stairs. They came bouncing in with many a laugh and joke, which Gilbert presently put an end to by saying, "Now, boys, here's a matter that concerns my honor. I'm responsible for Perry Kent in this room, and Barry here suspects him of stealing. Now, to satisfy us, I want you to declare, on your honor, whether you know anything about this pencil. We shall find out that it's a joke, I expect, before we're half through. Do you know anything about it, Turner?"

Turner replied that on his honor he did

not, and looked somewhat offended, as if his honesty was questioned. Bob Upham made the same answer, as did Ray Hunter. So, one after another, the rest affirmed the same thing, till there was no one left unquestioned but Tom Fowler. Matters began to look serious. Gilbert was firm, but at heart he trembled. He put the question to Tom, almost expecting to see him burst into a laugh and acknowledge the whole; but Tom denied all knowledge of the affair quite as gravely as the rest. Gilbert shivered as he said, "Ray, open the window and tell Perry I want to see him."

Ray did as he was desired, and after the lapse of a few minutes the boy came running into the room, expecting to see no one but his protector, but instead, finding all the first class ranged about the room, and regarding him curiously. His eyes fell, and his color rose.

There was a strange wavering betwixt tenderness and coldness in Gilbert's voice as he said, " Perry, come here. Barry White, in this chair by me, misses his gold pencil, which he left on the table out yonder. All these fellows know nothing about it. Now we want to know if you've seen it."

" Ask him if he's taken it," said Bob Upham, in a disagreeable tone.

Gilbert gave the speaker a look which said a great deal in a quiet way, and then added, " Yes, it comes to the same thing, Perry; have you stolen Barry White's pencil?"

# CHAPTER XI.

UNDER A CLOUD.

THOUGH the eyes of all the Boat Club were upon him, regarding his crimson cheeks and downcast eyes as sure signs of guilt, yet, when Gilbert asked this plain question, something within the little boy's heart enabled him to raise his eyes to Gilbert's own, and say, with more spirit than he had ever before displayed, —

"No, I haven't stole it."

"Well, did you ever hear anything like that?" said Tom Fowler; "he denies it, and uses bad grammar into the bargain."

"Wait," said Gilbert, looking at Tom;

then to Perry, with a distressed manner, "Haven't you seen it either?"

"No," said his protege, as spiritedly as before.

The room grew perfectly still, all waiting to see what Gilbert would do.

Captain Starr had never felt so distressed before. Here was the boy whom he had believed and trusted in as something better, purer, nearer the true standard of what a boy should be than the whole of them; it was he who had first aroused a sense of unworthiness in his own heart; he who had unconsciously reproached him by his actions and motives every day; he who had delighted and surprised him with such strong gratitude and affection; and now, to have him charged with such guilt and meanness, and without the power to refute it, why, it shocked and appalled him. He almost doubted his own senses.

Perry looked up at him in this strange silence with a quick, searching gaze, as if he suddenly suspected that Gilbert doubted his word, and his protector's eyes fell and his face flushed.

"Oh, if I only knew," Gilbert thought to himself, — "if I only *knew!*"

At most times Perry's word would have determined his course; but now, with the honor of the whole class pledged against this little boy's word, he wavered. A suspicion crept into his mind that he had been this apparently pure-hearted boy's dupe; he might have adopted all this show of gentleness and simplicity in order to deceive. At another time these foolish suspicions would not have found a place in Gilbert's head for a moment; but now, so amazed and unsettled was he that he could not judge between the folly and truth of the matter, and said to himself again, "If I only *knew*, I wouldn't hesitate a moment!" But he could know no more, and here were Perry's word and the honor of the class, to decide between.

The Boat Club exchanged glances and smiled; it was something new to see their Captain in such distress and perplexity. To them the scene was quite diverting; only Albert Turner looked grim. Pretty soon he said, proudly, —

"I would like to know whether Captain Starr doubts the honor of his Club?"

"Sure enough," said Bob Upham; "I hadn't looked at it in that light before; it *does* look as if he hesitated between our word and that little snip's."

Ray Hunter crossed over and whispered in Gilbert's ear, —

"For Heaven's sake, Gil, don't put off another minute; it looks as if you doubted us all!"

"But," said Gilbert, "I'm not sure; I *can't* decide. It's a hard thing to make a mistake about. Oh, Ray, if you knew how I felt!"

But Ray returned in a whisper, "Show your courage! be a *man!* Why, you're going to shelter this little baby just because you like him! Is that the kind of justice for a head-boy to have?"

These words were not without their effect. Gilbert really began to think his protege guilty, and acted accordingly.

'Perry," said he, coldly, "you'll have to acknowledge that everything is against you. No other boys, out of the first class, ever come in here but you. My friends have all said, on their honor, that they know nothing about it, and I must believe them. Now—"

"Do *you* believe I'm guilty?" said Perry, falteringly.

Gilbert hesitated an instant, then said, "Yes, I believe you're guilty. I don't see how it can be any other way."

"Oh, Gilbert!" cried the boy, appealingly.

"Stop," said his protector; "it's no harder for you to bear than for me. I said I would be responsible for your conduct, and this is my reward. You've disgraced me, as well as yourself, and — and — oh, how I have been deceived!"

Gilbert left his chair and walked to the window. to hide something besides anger. When he came back, he found that his protege had sunk down upon the floor and hidden his face.

"That looks like guilt," thought he, with a shiver; but he was touched for all that, and said, in a softer tone, "If you'll confess the whole, and ask these boys' forgiveness, I'll think about smoothing the matter over. Be quick; for there's no time to lose. Speak, Perry,—give me an answer."

"I didn't do it," said Perry, brokenly.

"Stop; that's not true. Now will you confess the whole?"

"I can't; I didn't do it!" was all Perry would say.

"You *did* do it!" said his protector, stamping on the floor. "Will you confess it?"

No answer.

"The Captain's lamb is an obstinate thing," said Tom, in an audible whisper, at which the rest of the Club laughed.

Of course, this did not serve to lessen Gilbert's temper. What with his grief and disappointment, dismay at being thus deceived, and vexation at Perry's obstinacy, he almost lost himself in a fit of passion.

Raising his protege off the floor, he forced him into a chair with no light hand.

"Will you confess what you've done?" he asked, angrily,—"will you? Tell me! quick! I won't wait long."

Still no answer, and again the boys laughed.

Gilbert hurriedly asked the question again, and meeting with no better success, madly raised his hand to strike. Ray Hunter stepped between, and caught the blow on his own sturdy shoulders.

"There," said he, as he grasped Gilbert's hand, "you're getting beside yourself, old fellow. Stop and think!—you wouldn't strike that little fellow in your senses."

Gilbert did stop, and thought. His face crimsoned. He would not be a bully if the thing were never confessed! and touching Perry, he said, "Well, keep the secret if you like. It will harm yourself more than any one else, and you'll have a chance to display your obstinacy; but see here,"— growing fierce, — "I cast you off! I'm not responsible for you any longer, and you needn't claim my protection again. Keep away from me! — out of my sight; I don't want to see you."

He took Perry by the arm and led him into the hall, bidding him to go, and as the boy was about to obey, stooped down and whispered, "If it'll do you any good, you may know that I never was so deceived in my life. I'll never believe in anything good again!"

Then he went back to his comrades, looking very resolute.

"Well," said Bob Upham, approvingly, "you finished that matter up after the old fashion. You act more like yourself than I've seen you for a month."

"Who else have I acted like?" demanded Gilbert.

Upham was careful not to provoke Gilbert by answering, and taking no notice of him, the Captain said, "Now I've a favor to ask of all of you, and it is this: don't spread the news of this affair all over school. I don't care for myself, but this little fellow will get a heavy punishment enough without our adding to it, and, White, I'll make good the loss of your pencil, so the matter needn't go to Winterhalter's ears. Now what do you say?"

"Well," said Tom, with more feeling than Gilbert had ever seen him display before, "I agree to it. What's the use of hammering the little chap after he's down? He's got enough to do to keep up, after what Gilbert's said to him. Did you see?—he wilted right down after he found out that he thought him guilty. Yes! let's keep the matter to ourselves."

"Thank you, Tom," said Gilbert, warmly; "I don't want to see the boy ill-treated, though he has deceived me."

One after another, the rest of the Club acquiesced before the supper-bell rang and they hurried off. Gilbert did not go down; so, when Ray Hunter found it out, he went back up to their chamber and found the Captain in his chair before the window, with his head on the sash.

Now, to do Ray's heart justice, he was sincerely sorry for what had occurred. True, he disliked Perry because of his influence over his friend, and was not sorry to see it broken, but he was pained to see how Gilbert had been shocked and disappointed. He remembered, too, that he had just declared himself sick of their false way of living, and ready to commence a better course; and though he hardly sympathized with this, he could feel pity for the harsh thrust which dashed all Gilbert's hopes and aspirations to the ground. So he pulled away the Captain's hands from his face, stroking back his hair as tenderly as a boy could be expected to do, saying, " Come, where's your pluck and courage, old fellow? Worse things than this happen to folks. Why, did you think that little fellow was perfection itself?"

"Oh, Ray!" said Gilbert, "I don't believe there's a good person in the world!"

"Pshaw! yes, there is, — Mrs. Winterhalter for instance. And if you say that, I'll contradict you, for my mother is good. Now brighten up, and let Perry Kent take care of himself. He isn't worth thinking about."

" He *was* worth thinking about," said Gilbert; " he put some thoughts into my heart

which I'm sure were good, if there were
never any such there before."

" Then why not stick to 'em?" said Ray.

" That's very easy to ask," said Gilbert,
" but I tell you I haven't the heart for anything after this. I'm discouraged to try!
Perhaps you'll think that it's a poor longing to be better that can't stand alone, but
goes under at the first knock; but I can't
help it! It's so."

" There, Captain, I don't think any such
thing. You'll come out of this. What do
you want to be any better for? You're
good enough for *me*, now. You don't swear,
you don't bully, you don't chew nor smoke,
like some of Roth's boys, and you behave
like a gentleman. Come, do you suppose
I want you to go to getting any better
than you are now,—putting on your high-
heeled shoes and wearing a Quaker suit
and talking through your nose? No, sir!

Give me Gilbert Starr just as he is now, and I'll love him ten times better than when he's starched up into a *goody*, sanctimonious old Roundhead!  Old fellow, come down to supper."

Gilbert laughed a little at this, but did not look very cheerful.

"I wish Barry and his pencil were in Tartary, before ever they made trouble here," continued Ray; "and I wish, for your sake, that Kent wasn't a thief; but since we can't help ourselves, what's the use of sitting down here and spooneying over it?"

"You're right," said Gilbert, with a resolute face; "I'll live it down.  Keep my secrets for me, Ray, you blessed fellow, and I'll show them I don't mind it.  What's the use of trying to be good?  It's no use! and — and — "

Gilbert's eyes fell on the far, wide vista of summer hills, fair and golden · in the day's declining, and ended his sentence with a sigh.

"Stop that!" said Ray, the ever-watchful; "you'll go into a fit of melancholy in two minutes if you stand here looking at those yellow hills;" and straightway he threw one arm over Gilbert's shoulder, and drew him away.

They left the window and passed into the hall. Perry Kent stood there, leaning against the balusters, and as the two came out, he started toward his former protector with an appealing look and gesture; but Gilbert took no more notice of him than if he were the merest pebble upon the floor, and, arm in arm with his friend, passed down to supper.

Everybody at the supper-table said that Captain Starr had never been gayer or merrier. He joked with Tom Fowler as much as table-propriety would allow; he

had a word for Rufe Fitch and Sam Copp
even, and those two leaders of the lower
classes were in the best of spirits on that
account.  Ray Hunter opened his eyes very
wide at this unusual levity, and thought to
himself, "Poor Gil! he's making all this
fun; he don't feel a bit of it."

However, this merriment answered one
purpose which pleased Ray very well; it
made Gilbert popular, if it did not make
him happy.  He never was more popular
than when he went out to the lawn that
night, after supper, and the Boat Club had
never been so proud of him.

"Talk about Gilbert's not being a
good captain," said Tom Fowler, as he
watched Gilbert's motions from under the
ash tree; "why, he could rule a kingdom!"

The little boy, up-stairs by the balusters,
leaned over and felt tempted to throw him-

self down. He heard the trample of feet
as the school swept out to the lawn after
supper; he heard Gilbert's voice sound-
ing blithely among them, and when he remembered that the voice was not to be
kind and pleasant to him any longer, he
sat down on the floor and wept bitterly.
Gilbert hated him; ·Gilbert despised him;
Gilbert thought him a thief, and, worst
of all, · Gilbert had said that he never
would believe in anything good again!
He sat here, sobbing, till it began to grow
dusk in the long corridor, and still saw
no way by which he might prove his innocence. No one would take his word
before all the great boys in the first class;
no one would take time to listen to his
story; no one would take his part, now
that Gilbert was against him; so what
could he do? It grew darker and duskier,
but still he sat disconsolately upon the

floor, and the few boys who straggled through the hall failed to see him as they passed; but by and by there came a light step along the corridor, the soft rustle of a dress, and a pair of kind eyes saw what the boys had failed to discern.

"Dear me! what can the matter be?" was the first knowledge which Perry had of Mrs. Winterhalter's presence, and then the good lady lifted him up, leading him into the adjoining room, where sufficient daylight lingered to enable her to see whom she had found in trouble. "Perry Kent! and crying, too!" she exclaimed. "Why, my dear boy, what is the matter?"

The boy's troubles were not to be told in one breath, and before they were all disclosed Mrs. Winterhalter led him down to the parlor to hear the remainder. She looked very grave when he had finished.

"I am astonished at Gilbert," she said,

after a few minutes' thought; "and yet it's very strange about the pencil. He wouldn't have talked to you so unless he believed he was right. But *I* don't think so, my dear," with one of her cheerful smiles; "and now do you keep up a bright heart and face, and the Right will have to triumph at last. I'll see what I can do about it." With that, she let Perry go, and he went up to bed somewhat comforted in spirit.

"*God* knows," he thought, "that I didn't do it, and mamma knows, and he'll bring it right, sometime, just as Mrs. Winterhalter says. But if Gilbert——" To get past his friend's name without breaking down was an utter impossibility, and his pillow was wet with quite as bitter tears that night as were shed upon his first day at Rainford.

But this was not the hardest thing which

he had to bear. The Boat Club were true to their promise, and whispered the story of the theft to no one; but if Gilbert thought to prevent the boy from being persecuted by this precaution, he was utterly mistaken. The keen-eyed boys of the lower classes were not long in observing that Perry was no longer under Captain Starr's protection, and that he was even regarded with disfavor; therefore they pounced upon him at once, as an object for their sport and tyranny. Perhaps they intended to make up for lost time; at any rate, they gave the unfortunate boy little peace of his life. These things Gilbert saw every day, but hardened his heart, and, true to his promise, denied the victim any protection. "He didn't spare me," he would say to himself, when he felt impelled to take Perry's part, "and now I won't spare him." Sometimes Ray Hunter, whose heart was too warm to allow him to see downright cruelty practised, interfered and set the boy free from his captors; but Ray was rarely present on these occasions, and then Perry was obliged to shift for himself.

Two or three weeks passed. The affair of the pencil remained quite as much of a mystery to poor Perry as ever, and Gilbert was quite as much of an enemy. Was it any wonder that the boy began to grow discouraged?—that, between Gilbert's coldness and his schoolmates' tyranny, he grew fearful and wretched? If he ventured on to the lawn, there was no peace to be found there. Gilbert's stern face was almost always to be found in their chamber, and that was worse to endure than Sam Copp's persecutions.

During this time one thing occurred which touched Gilbert's heart exceedingly.

He was so unfortunate as to catch a duck-
ing while out boating.   The night was
cool, even · chilly.   He came home cold
and shivering, and went to bed to find
that Mrs. Winterhalter's summer coverlets
were hardly warm enough for a boy in his
condition.   But when he awoke the next
morning, it was to find that an extra blanket had been spread carefully over him.
Who could have done it?   A few minutes'
search with his eyes around the · room told
him who had slept that night without any
covering but a sheet.   He said nothing,
but restored the blanket 'to its owner's bed,
and for a few seconds could not help gaz-
ing at his sleeping protege through very
misty eyes.

# CHAPTER XII!

RACE NUMBER TWO.

THE middle of August came, and found Perry Kent still in disgrace, and suffering such persecutions as only sensitive little boys can suffer. He longed to leave school, but, homeless and friendless, there was no refuge to which he might flee. If it had not been for Mrs. Winterhalter's kindnesses, the little boy would certainly have yielded to his misfortunes and given himself up to the apathetic endurance of his troubles, caring naught for books or study; but the kind lady had ever a word of cheer and sympathy for the friendless little fellow whenever she met him,—which she took care should be often,—and she even went so far as to remonstrate with Captain Starr. But Gilbert was firm, and, though evidently touched by his protege's lonely, unprotected condition, would make no concession, not even when the good lady requested it as a particular favor to herself. "He's deceived me," Gilbert had said, "and now I don't want anything to do with him."

"But," Mrs. Winterhalter replied to this, "suppose you are in the wrong? Now I have no more suspicion that Perry is guilty of theft than I have that you are. Isn't it a cruel thing to keep him in such a wretched condition?"

Gilbert was incredulous, and attributed the good lady's faith in Perry's innocence to her "good-heartedness," as he termed it; and so day after day went by, till August began to wane.

Then there came a new subject of comment and speculation for the Rainford boys. Perry heard the boys of his class eagerly discussing the matter, and little by little came to know what it was all about. But the whole substance of the matter was this: Albert Turner came to Gilbert on one of the August evenings, and placed a note in his hand, saying,—

"Here's something you'd like to read, Captain. Wait, I'll read it for you. Fred Moore came over with it."

The Boat Club, hearing Moore's name mentioned, gathered around to hear their secretary read,—

"RIVERSIDE, Tuesday Eve, August 25.

"The RIVERSIDE CLUB present their compliments to the EAST-SIDE CLUB, and respectfully challenge them to race with the boats next Saturday afternoon. Mr. Prescott holds the prize-flag yet, and will endeavor to award it to Captain Starr's satisfaction. If the Club are inclined to accept, Captain Forrest would like to meet Captain Starr on Rainford bridge to-morrow night, with *peaceful intentions.*

"Respectfully,

"RIVERSIDE CLUB."

"Well, that's cool and impudent," said Ray; "after what has happened, I should think Forrest had better keep a civil tongue in his head. Did you hear that, Captain? He wishes to meet you with *peaceful intentions!* That's Forrest's work, plainly."

"Yes," said the secretary, "Forrest always writes his own notes, and puts what he pleases into them. And—do you see?

—he thinks Mr. Prescott will award the flag to Captain Starr's satisfaction."

"Forrest is smart; you can't deny that," said Tom; "and for my part, I'd like another tussle with his men. We shall be pretty apt to bring the flag back with us."

"It *is* a shame that our flag should be that side of the river," said Barry White.

"Well, what do *you* think?" Ray said, turning to Captain Starr; "we're all waiting to hear."

"I said I'd never race with them again," said Gilbert, looking over the note; "but I was mad then; and I *would* like to whip Forrest and get our flag again. Next Saturday. Let me see, this is Tuesday evening. There'll be three evenings for practice yet, and we make pretty good time now. I think we can beat them."

"So do I!" cried Tom, enthusiastically; "and even if we can't, don't let's allow our flag to be a prisoner without making a dash for it. I go in for the race."

The Club seemed to be unanimous in this declaration of Tom, and Gilbert was not decidedly averse to racing.

"Has Moore gone back?" he asked.

"I left him by the hedge-gate," Al Turner said.

"I'll go and see," said Tom, hurrying off.

"If he is here yet," said Gilbert, "you shall write an acceptance, Al, and send it back by him. Tell Forrest I'll meet him with *peaceful* intentions, and say we accept Saturday for the day, and so on."

The secretary ran off to his room to write the note, and hardly was he out of sight before Tom came back, saying,—

"I've found him; he was just going down the lawn to his boat, and I stopped him. He says he'll wait five minutes for Al to do his scribbling in."

Within that time the note was written and despatched to the challengers. So the matter was decided, and there was another race in prospect.

Most boys like excitement and novelty, and Mr. Winterhalter's were no exception. They received the news with cheers, and thought Captain Starr a "splendid fellow," and "good for Forrest any day."

On the following night, Gilbert went to the appointed place to meet his rival. When he came in sight of the long stone bridge, and heard the waves lapping the piers, saw the sky stained crimson, the river flashing back its hues far up and down its silvery reach, he remembered, with something like a sigh, how on just such an evening a little figure had followed him the long, long path, to throw itself in the way of his own wrong-doing. He even stopped and looked behind him, hardly knowing why he did so, yet half-expecting to see a boy's shadow flit out of sight.

Forrest was punctual, and the two captains met and shook hands with no show of dislike. There was even something like cordiality in the manner in which Forrest put his hands on Gilbert's shoulders, saying, good-humoredly,—

"Shall we be startled out of our senses by having a little fellow drop down upon us from the clouds to-night?"

"No," said Gilbert, gravely enough; "we sha'n't be molested this time, I'll warrant."

"But who was the little chap?" said Forrest; "he seemed wonderfully fond of you, anyhow."

"Pshaw! only a little fellow in our second class. Let's to business."

"Agreed," said Forrest, and to business they went.

When it was all over, and Gilbert was walking homeward through the darkening meadows, with the sky all sombre-suited, and the river rolling on · to the sea with many a plashing in the low willow boughs and the nodding •rushes, he remembered how a little figure had run along the same dark and winding path, with the fireflies waving about it, and the river-sounds filling its ears, and it was all for him.

"Oh," he sighed to himself, as he slowly wended his way, "how *could* he deceive me so? I might have been a different fellow now, but for that. It's strange; I can't understand it at all,—he was so pure-hearted and simple, I thought. And I can see he loves me yet,"—remembering how he had been covered . up in the night, —"though how he can is a mystery. Oh, dear! what can a fellow do?"

There was boat-practice the next two

evenings,—plenty of it. Gilbert had some trouble to get his men in at nine o'clock, they were so anxious for the work; but he did it, and Mr. Winterhalter was pleased on account of it. Perhaps this was the reason why he granted the Captain liberty to leave his lessons at three o'clock, Friday afternoon, and spend the remainder of daylight on the river with his crew.

They came up the dew-drenched lawn that night at nine, boisterous and merry enough, and quite confident of winning their flag on the morrow.

"We're in better practise than ever before," Gilbert had said, and so they all thought; and Tom had been cracking jokes, at Mr. Winterhalter's expense, about their three weeks' strife for perfect lessons.

"Why," said he, boisterously, "put Gilbert Starr against Mr. Winterhalter, and we win every time! Wouldn't the old fellow scratch his head in amazement to know how I got such magnificent lessons for three weeks on a stretch? And — did you notice, the other day?—he turned back to those very lessons for a review in mathematics, and, of course, I couldn't have told a word about them if I was to swing for it. Didn't he stare! Ha, ha, ha! I thought I should laugh in his very face. But he said something about my having a 'relapse' or some such thing, and so passed on."

Now Gilbert could not bear joking upon this subject. The words stung him. He felt mean and degraded whenever he thought of the affair; so he replied, quickly, —

"Never say another word about that matter, Tom; I won't hear it! I think of it often enough without having you bawl it into my ears."

" Why, what ails it?" Tom asked, quite as quickly.

"It was your own plan," said Bob Upham.

"I know that," Gilbert answered; "but that don't make it any better. It was a mean trick to serve Mr. Winterhalter, any-how. It was a downright lie!"

"*Lie!*" "*Mean!*" hissed the club, indignantly.

"Yes; both of them. I didn't think of it at first, but I think so now. There was no honor about it."

Ray, who was a peacemaker for policy's sake, now interposed with a question to Tom, which quite turned that young gentleman's thoughts from dispute.

"Well," thought Ray, as they all went up-stairs to bed, "Gilbert's thinking just as much as ever, though he pretends not to be; and by and by he'll just boil over with his new notions, and then there'll be a terrible row! The boys'll fight against 'em, he'll stick to 'em like death, and down he'll come with a great crash, and — oh, *dear!* I wish I knew what to do with the fellow." And when, after all the rest were abed and the lamp was out, he chanced to look up from his pillow and saw in the dim light that Gilbert had not retired, but sat on the foot of his bed in an apparently deep reverie, he got up in sheer desperation and pattered across the floor to say,—.

"Now, Gil, *do* go to bed like a good fellow, and stop your everlasting thinking. You'll think yourself crazy, and there'll be a pretty muss! You aren't ready to go? Then I won't go, either, but I'll sit here just to bother you and stop your thinking-machinery. I don't care if you don't like it; if you won't take care of yourself, I suppose I've got to make up my mind to the task;" and with that he was as good as his word, and sat down beside Gilbert with a mock sigh of resignation.

Gilbert held his temper, and after a long silence, said, —

" Well, I suppose you mean well, Ray, but you've a queer way of showing it, sometimes.　I wish you'd let me alone, but since you won't, I'll go to bed.　Are you satisfied?"

"Yes, or will be when I see you keep your promise," and would not leave till he saw Gilbert's head on the pillow.

Saturday dawned quite as clear as did the day of the first race.　As there was no school on the last day of the week, the boys were at liberty to choose their own time for the race; accordingly, the hour had been set at ten in the forenoon.

As a particular favor, Mr. Winterhalter's boys were to be allowed to cross over to the Riverside shore, as there the best view could be obtained, and there were generally enough seats for all. To keep his community from quarrelling with their neighbors of the other shore, the gentleman himself, with some of the teachers, was to accompany them. Perhaps — it was rumored — Mrs. Winterhalter herself would go, and it was to be a general holiday for the schools and teachers of both sides.

With the prospect of such an array of spectators, you may be sure the Boat Club were more anxious than ever to redeem their flag. Numberless journeys were made between the lawn and the "Triton," in order to be certain that the boat lacked nothing necessary to make victory sure, and some of the Club were even dressed and ready before breakfast. At nine, the boats which always lay at the foot of the lawn were brought up to the wharf, and received their first loads, which were slowly ferried over. It was too long a walk, everybody thought, to go up to Rainford bridge, and so follow the river down the other side; and when boats were plenty, the river smooth, and oarsmen in abundance, why not ride?

Ned Rogers, who still had a patronizing word for Perry, searched everywhere till he found him in his old refuge under the syringas.

"Now," said he, with a very indignant expression, "if you aren't too bad to go and hide away in this style! I've a good mind not to show you what I've got for you." But presently he thought better of it, seeing that Perry had not much interest in the matter, and disclosed a bit of gay scarlet ribbon, the counterpart of a piece which fluttered from one of the button-holes of his jacket. "Look," he exclaimed, "and see what I've got for you! The boys will be all mixed up to-day, you know, and so our boys wear red in their button-holes, like the Club uniform, and Roth's boys wear blue. That's so we can tell who belongs to our side, you know. Now you wouldn't have had any if I hadn't made Gilbert give me two pieces when he was cutting up that long roll. Why don't you take it?"

"I'm not going to the race," said Perry, declining the offered badge.

"*Not going!* Why — what — how — Mrs. Winterhalter!" catching a glimpse of that lady's dress sweeping past the piazza-rail, "here's Perry Kent, and he says he isn't going to the race, when everybody's going, and there's going to be nobody left at home!"

"Is that so, Perry?" said the lady, stopping to look over. "Why, all the boys will be there, Mr. Winterhalter and I, the teachers, and the race will look nicely from Riverside. You will miss a great deal if you stay here. Come, tie the ribbon in your button-hole, and run down to the wharf with Ned."

Perry had not the least inclination to go, and would much rather have stayed in the quiet at home; but Mrs. Winterhalter said,—

"It's bad for boys to be always sitting still and not running about. Get your hat, Perry, and run down to the boat with Ned, — they're about to put off, — and go over to Riverside and enjoy yourself."

Perry did as he was ordered, and at ten o'clock found himself on a high wharf or platform, which ran out over the river, with a full view of the whole river-side and all its gay crowd.

The number of spectators at the first race was nothing in comparison with those now assembled. They filled all the benches along the water's edge, they sat in boats anchored a little way from shore, · they were crowded together upon the little wharves which pushed out from the river-edge. The school-boys were everywhere,—in the tree-tops, on the roofs of boat-houses, and crowded in among other spectators. Where Perry stood, there was a great number of his schoolmates, with a sprinkling of the Professor's blue-ribboned boys, and from their high station over the water they could look down upon the heads of those who had seats on the river-brink. Perry could see Mrs. Winterhalter down there, and—yes, actually with a red ribbon fluttering from the tip of her parasol!

Who would have thought it?  And next
her sat a large, richly-dressed lady, whose
parasol was likewise ornamented with ribbon, but its shade was blue instead of the
Rainford boys' color.  This lady, so Ned
presently whispered, was Mrs. Roth, and
that tall, stout man, a little behind her,
was the Professor himself, and by his side
stood Mr. Winterhalter, and there were
Rainford people all about them, some wearing one color and some another, and all
making a very gay sight.  People took a
great deal of interest in the boys' pleasures, after all, Perry thought.  He could
see Mr. Prescott stepping briskly about,
wearing a business-like face, while in his
button-hole the colors of the two Clubs
were blended, to show that he was partial toward neither.  The hum of conver-
sation grew louder and louder, till at last
it deepened into a cheer from the friends

of the Riverside Club as they rowed out and took their place. Gilbert's crew, of course, had to come from the other side, and as they advanced to the starting-place, were greeted with quite as warm a welcome as their rivals had been. A few more minutes of waiting and expectation, then the boats started. Forrest's friends on shore threw him back a parting cheer, as the "Mermaid" glided swiftly and gracefully down stream, and Gilbert's friends, on the high platform where Perry stood, not to be outdone, cheered him vociferously. Certainly, if the race could have been won by shouting, both boats would have stood nearly an equal chance for victory. But as it was to be won by hard pulling, the two crews bent their oars and sped away, the cheers serving to make them remember that some hundreds of hearts were wishing them victory.

The sun was not yet high enough to be oppressively warm, but it gilded the river like one long roadway of fretted silver, whereon the two black lines sailed down, one touched with red, the other with blue. Anxious eyes followed them, the more fortunate peering through spy-glasses; and when they were so far down that to the naked eye they did not seem to move, but lay motionless, those who had aids to their vision reported that they had turned the stake-boat, and the "Mermaid" seemed to have the start.

# CHAPTER XIII.



BACK up the river, with steady strokes, came the boats, eagerly watched by the hundreds of eyes on shore as they slowly began to assume size and proportion. A whisper had flown to the ears of Gilbert's friends that the "Mermaid" was ahead, and none were more eager than they to discover the truth of the rumor. Rufe Fitch even had the courage, under the circumstances, to go down from the high platform where he stood, and beg a look at the boats through Mr. Winterhalter's spy-glass, that he might report to the anxious gazers who were huddled together with him.　The Principal granted his request, and Rufe went back to his friends, jubilant.

"It's no such thing," he said, in reply to the questioning faces which were turned toward him as he scrambled back on the platform; "Gilbert's plump up with 'em, and not lagging a bit!　They've got so far back that I could see as plain as day through the glass.　Hurrah for our side!"

On and up till the oars began to gleam ruddily, till the drops began to sparkle, and they could see the rowers bending to their task with a will.　Both boats abreast, and each striving to gain a few inches, working, as only boys will work, for victory and honor.

"Oh," said Sam Copp, excitedly, "but Gil's got to stir himself if we get our flag!　It's only Tom Fowler's arms that can save us now."

So all Mr. Winterhalter's boys thought, and even the Principal himself observed, smilingly, to the Professor,—

"It bids fair to be an even race, sir. Abreast, and not many hundred yards more. My·head-boy will feel terribly mortified to have to leave the flag behind."

But it was quite certain that Mr. Winterhalter did not understand Tom Fowler as well as his pupils did, for they gazed breathlessly at the racers, confidently expecting to see their Captain's boat shoot ahead on the last hundred yards. What anxious waiting it was! How the owners of the blue and red ribbons looked defiantly in each other's faces, each confident of the other's discomfiture!

"Oh, why don't the 'Triton' begin to gain?" cried Rufe Fitch, almost in despair; "there can't be more than a hundred yards left!"

"It isn't going to gain at all," said one of the blue-ribboned fellows who stood by; "you'll see it drop behind pretty quick."

But Rufe was belligerent, and would listen to no such words, and the red-ribbons being in the majority on the platform, the rival party were obliged to keep their enjoyment to themselves.

"They're just abreast!" "Both come in at the same time." "Well-matched!" etc., were the exclamations which trembled on everybody's lips. Just then Captain Starr's boat suddenly shot a little ahead—merely a trifle—but the next stroke told so perceptibly that his friends on shore were in ecstasies. It seemed as if Tom Fowler had been waiting for just such an emergency as this to show his strength, for now every stroke carried the boat a little in advance of the "Mermaid," and

Forrest's crew could not keep their places. The red-ribboned boys were exultant.

"Hurrah for Tom Fowler!" cried Rufe, gleefully throwing up his hat; and chiming in with him, the friends of the "Triton" made the river-side ring. Tom, out on the river, heard it, and nerved himself for one last grand effort, saying, "Now for it, boys!"

The spectators watched eagerly, Forrest's friends hoping to see his crew gain their lost ground; but they were disappointed, for his men had been rowing their best for the last quarter-mile, and could do nothing better. So, on the last stroke, the "Triton" swept in grandly past the stakes, a full half-length ahead, and won the victory!

Then, you may be sure, there was a shout. Up and down Riverside the hurrahs rang, the handkerchiefs fluttered, and hands were clapped in applause. And when the first burst had died away, Mr. Winterhalter's boys took it up and made the welkin ring again, which last shout was more an exultation over their blue-ribboned rivals than for the victors.

The Roth boys looked chagrined and disappointed. They had counted on their Captain's success as certain, and now he had lost the race by half a length! It was too bad, they thought, and the victorious cheers grated on their ears.

Professor Roth laughed good-humoredly, at the defeat of his boys, and hinted that he must try and persuade that wonderful oarsman to take up his abode on the Riverside bank of the town. "And, by the way, who is he?" he inquired.

"I really don't know," said Mr. Winterhalter, smiling at his own ignorance; "I didn't know we had such a powerful-armed fellow in school. Rufus," to the boy above on the platform, " to whom are we indebted for this victory?"

" Tom Fowler!" said Rufe, not in a whisper, by any means; "he's the fellow that did it. Hasn't he got arms, sir?" And then Tom's name was whispered about among the crowd and praised in a manner that would have gratified him vastly, could he have heard it; but it was quite as well that he could not, since he had already a sufficiently high opinion of his strength and prowess.

Perry witnessed Gilbert's victory from his high station over the water, with a glad heart. It was pleasant to have him a victor, though he hated and despised himself, and he wished, with a suddenly heavy heart, that he might tell him how glad he was at the success, that he might rejoice and be merry with him, as Gilbert would once have been happy to have him do. He looked down in the cool, dark depths of the river under him, wishing sorrowfully that there was some refuge — a home, such as other boys had — where he might flee from all this suspicion and disgrace and persecution, and be quiet and happy. And oh, if mamma were only back to comfort him and tell him what to do! Perhaps she knew, perhaps she saw, and longed to comfort him, and knew *when* the end of this dark, dark day would be, he thought; and God *did* know, and would bring all right sometime; but, oh! *when* was the end to be? How could a weak little boy bear it any longer?—bear the neglect and loathing, the tyranny, the disappointment of waiting for days which brought no trace of the mystery's solution?

The victors and vanquished rowed shoreward side by side, amid the applause of the whole assembly. Boys never tire of cheering, at least the Rainford boys never did, and thought they could not shower too many honors upon Captain Starr and his crew. The two Clubs made a pretty sight as they came slowly up to the point where Mr. Prescott stood unfurling the crimson flag, preparatory to making his speech, the bright shadows of their jaunty uniforms trailing below them in the water, oar keeping stroke with oar, and, as they came up to the landing, Forrest politely fell back and allowed his victorious rival to take precedence.

"You may have the strongest boys," said the Professor's wife to Mrs. Winterhalter, as she observed this, "but I think our head-boy will out-rank them all for politeness."

"Perhaps so," said that good lady, with a smile; "yet I have seen our Gilbert

Starr do some brave things." And presently the Professor's wife had reason to agree with her.

As the boats came to a stand-still, there was a great stir among the crowd to get where they could see the presentation and hear what Mr. Prescott would say. The two principals' ladies left their chairs, and stood as near the railing at the river-edge as possible, and the Professor and Mr. Winterhalter were near by, looking over. Behind them the crowd pressed up close, a confusion of heads and faces, all anxious to see and hear. Mr. Prescott shook out the handsome pennon, gave the necessary "Ahem!" and opened his mouth to speak.

Just then the crowd on the high platform over the river pressed forward to get a better view, pushing and elbowing as only boys will, and clamoring for the best place.

"Here, get out of the way, Sam," said Rufe Fitch; "I can't see through your head."

"I can't stir, there's such a crowd!" said Sam; and spying Perry, who had a good, though rather pressed position, against the rail,—which was the only protection from tumbling off,—he exclaimed, "Here, you Perry Kent! get out o' that, and let me have that place. I want to see what's going on."

Probably he would have forced Perry away, had sufficient time been given him, but at that instant there was a warning crack and tremble of the railing, it shook, wavered, gave away, and before he could realize what had happened, Perry felt himself without support, falling — with a quick, awful shiver benumbing him from head to foot — down, down, down!

That crash stopped the words on Mr.

Prescott's lips. All eyes were turned in the direction of the sound just in time to see the crowd of boys fall back, and two figures topple over. A great hush, broken only by one shrill scream from Mrs. Roth's lips, fell instantly on the crowd on the river-bank; there was a splash and spatter of the water, then an awful silence, then two white faces came up to light and air after what had seemed an age. One of the figures threw up its hands, and after a few wild efforts, went through with the motions of swimming, and floated; the other went down almost as soon as it had seen the light.

The men on the bank, you must remember, were shut in by the railing and the crowd; and it had all happened so suddenly that every one's senses seemed to have forsaken him.

Captain Starr's boat was nearest the spot,

and perhaps he alone, of all the spectators, knew whose face it was that came up and sank so suddenly. Without a thought, before any one else had recovered their presence of mind, and so swiftly that no one really saw who it was, the " Triton" had shook from stem to stern, and a red-jacketed figure flashed down into the dark, shadowy water, out of sight. Mrs. Winterhalter gasped out to her husband, —

" That — that — was — was Gil — " and here lost her voice entirely. The Professor's wife sank down by her side, hiding her face, and the whole crowd were fairly breathless in those swift seconds.

The red jacket came up panting, with one scarlet arm thrown about a little figure, and after a few seconds of bobbing up and down and catching for breath, slowly struck out for shore with its burden.

Then there was help enough! Now that

the crisis was past, and the danger nearly over, people bethought themselves and began to stir. Somebody got over the railing and pushed out with a boat to meet the rescued and rescuer; and then Mrs. Winterhalter exclaimed, in a voice trembling with thankfulness,—

"It's Gilbert Starr, and he's saved Perry Kent!"

The man in the boat took the limp, drenched figure from Gilbert's hold, and laid it down on the floor.

Then Captain Starr swam back to the other figure, which was none other than Sam Copp, and succeeded in aiding the frightened and bewildered boy up to the boat's side, and over. Then, with the aid of the boatman, Gilbert clambered in all wet and dripping, and by this time fatigued enough with his exertions and the weight of his soaked clothes. Copp sank down

RESCUE OF PERRY KENT.  Page 270.

on the boat's bottom, looking faint and ex-
hausted. Something bright and glittering
slid from his pocket as he did so, and
rolled into the puddle of water which gathered from their trickling garments. Gilbert saw it, picked it up, and mechanically
put it in his pocket, without thinking or
looking to see what it might be; and, as
they touched the stone steps on the river-
edge, he took Perry up and sprang out.
A hundred hands were ready to take his
burden, — it seemed as if almost that number caught and helped him up the steps.
The first person he saw was Mrs. Winterhalter, tears and smiles struggling for the
mastery in her face. "Oh, Gilbert!" was
all she could say, and threw her arms about
his wet shoulders as if she had been his
own mother. Then the Professor's wife
stood next to greet him, and then the Professor himself and Mr. Winterhalter got

each a hand, and spoke so many earnest, thankful words that Gilbert began to think he had done something. Somehow, there were so many crowding about him, it was quite impossible to get beyond those stone steps. People wanted to shake hands and congratulate him, and would have their own way, and so he leaned against the railing and shook hands till his arm ached, and received so much praise and admiration that, at any other time, he might have suffered by it. But he felt very sober now, and not at all elated. He shivered when he thought of Perry Kent, and wondered where they had carried him.

"Give me your hand, Starr!" said Mr. Prescott, making his way through the crowd; "such an act is worth more than all the boat victories in the universe!" and it seemed as if he would never have done shaking and pressing the Captain's hand.

Then there came some of the Rainford town-people to see him, and a great crowd of the lower classes in his own school, and quantities of Roth's boys, till he began to despair of getting away unless he beat a retreat back to his own boat. And as he turned about with some such thought in his head, Ray Hunter came bounding up the steps from the "Triton," having lost his patience waiting for the Captain's return. Ray's eyes actually sparkled through tears.

"Thank God, you're safe and sound, old fellow!" he cried; "I thought I'd looked my last at you for two seconds. Gil, I say, — what a fellow you are! — and ain't I proud of you! Why, this is a perfect ovation!"

Ray kept his friend's wet hand, and stood by him all through the remainder of the crowding to see the Captain, and was

as proud and happy as though all the honor
was his own.

Mrs. Winterhalter came back to Gilbert
presently, saying, —

"Perry has revived, and is a great deal
better; he's shocked, more than injured,
the doctor says. Mr. Winterhalter has ordered a carriage to take him home, and
we want you to go, — you look tired
enough to, I'm sure."

Before he could reply, there came a great
cry of "Starr!" "Starr!" and, looking
up, there was Mr. Prescott waiting for him
to come up after the flag. Gilbert had actually forgotten all about it!

"Thank you; but I'll go home in the
'Triton,'" he said, and was about to hurry
away, when the good lady gently detained
him.

"You can't go now, I see," she said,
"and I'm sorry we can't stay to see you

take the flag; but haven't you a word now
for — for that little fellow you saved from
death?"

Gilbert's heart said quickly, "Forgive
him! — send him a kind word;" but from
his lips, "I can't! — *don't ask me!*" and
then he hurried off to receive his flag in
answer to repeated calls from all directions.

How the shouts and cheers went up as
he stepped before Mr. Prescott! The whole
river-side rang, and the applause came from
every one's lips, — from Forrest and his
crew as well, — and when he heard it, Mr.
Prescott gave up all thoughts of a speech.
What good could a speech do? Wet, dripping, with his uniform clinging to his limbs,
Gilbert stood there, not an elegant figure,
to be sure, but a hero in everybody's eyes!

After this presentation the crowd dis-
persed rapidly. Boat after boat-load of

Mr. Winterhalter's boys were ferried across the river. Gilbert, by this time, was getting chilly and weary, and glad enough that it was time to go home. As he came down the stone steps to take his place in the "Triton," he met Forrest, who was just landing from his own boat. The Professor's head-boy gave him a hug, regardless of his nice blue jacket.

"You and I can't afford to be enemies if we *are* rivals," said he, earnestly enough. "I'm proud to have you whip me at racing. Why, my fellows didn't think you was made of such stuff, but now I expect I shall lose my rank unless I do something that's equal to it in their eyes! And," he added, laughing, "what a propensity that little fellow has for coming down steep places; but he'd have drowned, as sure as a shot, but for you. Come, say we're friends, and let's stick to it."

Gilbert took Forrest's offered hand, and then got into his boat, where his friends gave him a boisterous welcome; then they rowed homeward as fast as possible, for the Captain's teeth began to chatter, even though the sun shone warm and full upon him.

# CHAPTER XIV.

## MAKING RESTITUTION.

AT the little wharf Gilbert's friends were congregated, waiting for him to return. Never had Mr. Winterhalter's boys been prouder of their leader, or more anxious to show their delight and affection; so, when he stepped from the "Triton," they gathered about him, not boisterous or clamorous, but quite soberly, expressing their feelings by warm grasps of the hand, or in those frank, blunt words which are generally at the end of boys' tongues. Ray, proud and happy, stood by his friend, and thought Gilbert had never looked so handsome and manly as at that moment and in that drenched and clinging uniform. It became him better, he thought, than a prince's rich garments and royal garb could ever have done. Then he remembered that it would never do for him to stand there in such a wet plight, and turning hastily to the boys, exclaimed,—

"Come, this never'll do. Don't you see the Captain's freezing to death while you're shaking hands and chattering so? Come, Gil, you'll catch your death of cold. Let the hand-shaking and all that sort of thing go till you're warm and dry." And with this he pulled his friend away and hurried him up the lawn, the boys straggling after them.

The carriage which conveyed Mr. and Mrs. Winterhalter and Perry from Riverside, rolled away from the front entrance just as the two came on to the lawn.

Gilbert shivered harder than ever when he saw it, remembering how near death his former protege had been, thinking how that white face looked as it came up through the dark water, wondering what prompted him to throw himself after it so suddenly. If it had not been for his cold, shivering state, his trickling garments, and the sense of fatigue which caused him to lean on Ray's good arm, it would all have seemed but a dream to him. The pale, appealing face flashing suddenly into sight, his own quick spring after it down into the dark and bubbling depths, the seconds of buffeting the water with his burden,— all seemed to him now like the vague, indistinct actions of a half-forgotten dream.

The two went in at the front-door, as it stood wide open and offered a shorter route to their room, and as they passed the study-door, caught a glimpse of a still motionless little figure on the sofa. Gilbert's heart beat fast, and he longed to enter, to say the words which his heart prompted; but his pride got the better of this tenderness, and so he went on, smothering the sigh which struggled up ·to his lips. Just as they were leaving the hall to go up-stairs, Mrs. Winterhalter came in on her way to the study with blankets and flannels. She smiled sweetly to Gilbert, saying, —

"Hurry and get off your wet clothes, dear," but said not a word about Perry.

"Yes," said Ray, as the good lady hurried on, "you sha'n't loiter another second. Come, hurry up with you, and get off these soaked things. Seems as if we never should get here. You're getting as white as the wall, and your teeth, — goodness! how they chatter! And—and, Gil, do look behind you at the stream of water that is running down-stairs.   Why, we might have rowed you up here in the 'Triton' if we'd only thought."

They entered their room, and Ray locked the door.

" Now don't you lift your finger, old fellow," he said, . bustling about; " I'll get these things off you in a twinkling, and then for such a rubbing as you haven't had in one six months.   If it don't put some color and warmth into you, then I'll give up.   Gracious! how your shoes stick, and, if you'll believe me, there's at least half a pint of water in 'em!   What a lucky chance this'd be for the washwoman, if it was only Monday!   I've a good mind to let you be till then; 'twould fill up her wash-tubs so. nicely, and save such a sight of pumping.   Let your jacket alone; .I'll 'tend to it in a minute."

So Ray bustled about, busy and helpful.

He soon removed his friend's wet clothing, wrung out his dripping locks, and rubbed him with towels till his natural warmth began to return and glow delightfully in all his veins. Gilbert took it all passively enough, and as he grew warm and comfortable under Ray's ceaseless rubbing, thought gratefully to himself that there was not such another friend in the whole world wide, and wondered regretfully how he could ever have had the heart to give him such harsh words as he had sometimes done.

At last Ray ceased his exertions, warm and panting. "How do you feel now, old fellow?" he asked, looking up brightly.

"As warm as — a toast," said Gilbert, gratefully; "now for dry clothes, and then I'll be as good as new."

"Wait a bit, till I've combed your hair;

it's wringing wet yet, and wants a good rubbing and brushing."

So Ray turned barber for the occasion, and gave his friend's head a creditable shampooing, brushed the damp locks up from his forehead, made experiments with a view to seeing whether his hair looked best brushed before or behind his ears, and with a last flourish pronounced Gilbert to be "beginning to look like himself."

Then came dry garments which felt luxuriously warm and nice, and when he had got on his blouse, and was dry and comfortable from head to foot, he declared that he felt "better than before; and it's all owing to you, Ray, you best of friends, and I'll never forget it as long as I live. Now let's go down to the lawn and stir about a little, for I do feel just the least bit sleepy and stupid."

Ray had seated himself on the foot of

a bed opposite his friend, whom he was regarding half-dreamily; and Gilbert himself fell into a reverie, instead of going down to the lawn as he had proposed. Ray presently broke the silence by saying,—it was a continuation of the thoughts running in his own brain at that moment,—

"When I saw you spring past us, right out into the water, and down, down, like a piece of lead, I thought it was your last dive. I thought—oh, Gilbert! I shiver when I think of it. And it was all for Perry Kent."

"Or for any one else, had they chanced to be in his predicament," said Gilbert, with a shadow on his face.

"Yes, I know. You'd go right in if 'twas boiling pitch, without a thought for yourself; and some of these days you'll lose your life, and then you'd better have looked out for Number One."

"You don't mean that," said Gilbert, looking keenly at his friend; " you'd never stand by and see a little fellow drown before your eyes,— or a big one either, for that matter. Why, who jumped in, too, when I fell out of the 'Triton' one night, and got me by the arm, when the water was hardly up to our chins, and I swim like a fish?" and Gilbert laughed merrily at the remembrance of Ray's fright and anxiety.

"Well, I *was* frightened that time," Ray admitted, "and I did not know what shallow water 'twas, you see; but that don't prove anything, for when you get into trouble, I just don't think, somehow, and plump overboard. But it's different with the rest, and if it had been Perry Kent, and he had deceived me as he did you, I don't know but I should have — have let —"

"Pshaw!" said Gilbert, "I know you better than that, and besides, I don't want to talk about Perry. Let's drop the subject, and go down. I hear the fellows on the lawn."

"Well, I'm ready. Now you look like yourself once more, old fellow,—better than I should think you could after such a day's work. But here"—as they were leaving the room,—"here's your uniform all soaked and dripping. It'll spoil, so. Let's carry it down to Mrs. Brant. She'll fix it up as bright as a new pin."

"There's things in the pockets," said Gilbert; "we'd better take those out."

Ray thrust his hand into the wet depths and drew out a knife. Then came a soaked handkerchief, then a pocket-book whose contents were somewhat the worse for water, and then something at the sight of

which Ray staggered back a little, exclaim
ing, —

" What ! — Gilbert, why, this — this —
this is — good heavens ! how came *this* in
your pocket, Gilbert Starr ? "

It fell from Ray's hand, and Gilbert
stooped quickly and picked it up. It was
Barry White's long-missing pencil, as
bright and new as when it disappeared,
and on one end were the engraved letters,
B. W., as plain as were ever letters in the
world. Gilbert looked up to his friend
with wide-open, astonished eyes.

" What does this mean ? " he exclaimed,
bewildered.

" If *you* can't tell, how can I ? " said
Ray, with eyes quite as wide open as Gilbert's.

Captain Starr looked down at the pencil,
then at his friend, then back at the pencil,

with a very troubled and puzzled countenance.

"Don't you know?— can't you think?"
said Ray. "Why, it couldn't have been
done by magic."

"It was, for all that I know to the con-
trary," said Gilbert, in utter perplexity.

"But think, Gilbert," said Ray; "sit
down and think, and perhaps you'll remember some fact, or something that'll
help you. Could Kent have put it in your
pocket?"

Gilbert sat down in the seat which he
had just vacated, and, without answering his
friend's question, covered his face and tried
to think. Suddenly he looked up to Ray,
the color all fleeing from his face, and exclaimed, huskily,—

"Ray, I see it all now! This pencil fell
out of Copp's pocket when I helped him
into the boat. I saw it shine, and picked

it up without noticing or thinking whose pencil it was, and thought I would give it to him when we got to shore. But I forgot it, — forgot all about it, and now — oh, Ray! Perry Kent is just as *innocent of that theft as you or I!*"

Ray dropped down on the foot of the bed, and stared blankly. Gilbert was white and silent for a few minutes, then burst out with, —

"Oh, Ray Hunter, what *have* I done? Don't you see? — that little fellow is as innocent as a lamb, and I have — have —"

Gilbert's voice sank lower and lower, till it died away in a whisper, and he looked down at the floor so remorsefully that Ray's senses came back to him.

"You don't just know, old fellow," said he, quickly; "there may be some mistake, and don't kill yourself till you're certain."

"Certain? I am certain!" cried Gilbert; "and, oh, what shall I do? I've been the cruelest wretch! I've been — I — oh, Ray! I can't tell you what I've been. It makes me wild to think of it!"

"Wait and think," said Ray, consolingly. "Don't you see you're not so much to blame? All the Boat Club against that little fellow, and you to decide between 'em. How could you help it?"

"Oh, but I might have known!" said Gilbert, remorsefully; "he never deceived me in the world, and I ought to have taken his word, even if the whole Club came down upon me, and oh, why didn't I?"

"Because you couldn't see any further through a millstone than anybody," said Ray, comfortingly; "you couldn't be expected to know everything; and it was only a common enough mistake, such as anybody might make. And I dare say Perry hasn't minded it much."

"That's because you don't know him," said Gilbert, after a long, long silence, in which his pale and downcast face had greatly troubled Ray. "Don't you think I could see how he suffered when the boys tormented him? Don't you think I knew how it wounded him when, I turned him off? Wouldn't it have hurt you to be suspected of theft, and lose all your friends in consequence? Oh, but I know and have seen it all, and I — I —"

"Now stop!" said Ray, vehemently. "What's the use? You've saved his life this very day, and if that doesn't more than make up for what he's 'endured,' then there's no hope for you."

"And I refused to give him a kind word not ten minutes after!" said Gilbert, with a fresh pang of regret, — "and if I had failed, — if anything had happened that I missed my hold of him in the water, and he had gone down for the last time — oh, Ray, it's horrible to think of! He would have drowned, and I should have had all my cruelty to think of as long as I lived."

"Pshaw!" said Ray; but he looked exceedingly uncomfortable for all that.

Presently Gilbert got up quickly, and walked toward the door, and, to his friend's question, "Where are you going?" replied, "Down to the study."

Gilbert's heart beat very fast as he went down-stairs, and his cheeks, which had been so pale, now began to flush and crimson when he thought of his errand. He had got to humble himself, — confess to a degree of wrong and injustice which made his eyes fill to think of; and he had got to confess himself in the wrong, — terribly in the wrong, which seems to be a very hard thing for all boys to do. He came to the door, and there Mrs. Winterhalter caught sight of him, and left her seat by the sofa to see what he wanted.

"Why, Gilbert, what's the matter?" she exclaimed, as she noted his manner.

"Can I see—Perry?" he asked, his voice trembling.

The good lady looked at him keenly a minute, then a happy smile flitted over her face, and then she said, softly,—

"Yes, yes!—go in now. I know— don't stop to tell me, but go in!" and she stepped into the hall and closed the door after her, thus leaving Gilbert by himself.

Perry lay with closed eyes on the sofa, white and still; but at the sound of the new-comer's footsteps, which were hardly as soft as Mrs. Winterhalter's, he looked up, and saw—Gilbert. The quick color flashed into his wan face; he started up a little from his pillow, then sank back,

as pale as before and much distressed.
The next instant Gilbert was beside him, —
down on his knees, — his arms about him,
and he whispering, —

"Can you ever, ever forgive me, Perry
Kent?"

A half-smothered cry came from the little boy's lips as he put his arms about his
friend's neck, and then — how it was, Gilbert could not tell — it seemed as if the
great wretched gulf between them had
rolled away, and they were the same
friends as ever, only, at that moment,
both joyful and sorrowful at once!

Mrs. Winterhalter came in after a while,
and found Gilbert gone, and Perry sleeping peacefully. A few skilful questions,
when he awoke, revealed all to the good
lady, — all except the name of the real cul-
prit, and that the boy did not wish to disclose.

"I don't care," he had said, "now that Gilbert knows all about it, and we are such good friends again, and he will never, never doubt me again. And Gilbert has promised such good things; and oh, Mrs. Winterhalter, I am so happy! and the duck in the river was just nothing at all; for, you see, it told Gilbert who the real thief was, and it has made everything all bright and smooth once more. So, if you had just as lief, I would rather not tell."

From the study Gilbert went out to the lawn. He found Copp among the boys who thronged about him, and, taking him by the arm, whispered,—

"Sam, I want you up in my chamber a few minutes. Not a word, sir, but come on as I tell you," and led the boy away from his wondering classmates.

Gilbert led him in without a word, up

the stairs, pausing at the door of the chamber to say, —

" Now, Copp, if you're obstinate, and don't tell the plain truth, I'll turn you over •to those who can make you. Hold up your head, and come on," and with that ushered him in where the Boat Club were busy removing their uniforms and substituting their every-day suits.

"Here," said Gilbert, soberly, " is a fellow who has got something to say that will interest us all; " and holding up the pencil before Sam's wondering eyes, added, — .

" Now, begin at the beginning, and tell the whole. No halting, now. Go on!"

The Boat Club · suspended operations, and looked on in amazement. Copp looked nervously about him for a few seconds, then, seeing there was no help for him, began his confession. It was a confused and broken story, but the Club made out its significance.  He had coveted the pencil, and was shrewd enough to guess that the suspicion would rest upon Perry at once, and feeling secure from discovery, stole into the Club's chamber, one day, and removed it.

When he had finished, Gilbert said to his friends, —

"I've done a cruel thing, boys, and I'm ashamed of it.  I want you to treat Perry Kent well, for my sake, at least, and that's no more than his due.  You can go now, Copp.  You've had the satisfaction of seeing me act like a brute toward the little fellow you've wronged, and I want you to keep away from me for a while."

Sam made his escape, quite willing to perform Gilbert's requirement, and then the Captain sat down with his face to the window and his back to the boys, thinking what an eventful day it had been, and feeling very sober and thoughtful.

Perry had not deceived him, after all, and the thought was so pleasant that he lingered over it, thinking anew of many things which he had been trying to drive out of his head during those disagreeable weeks.

# CHAPTER XV.

## A NEW-COMER, AND FOREBODINGS.

WHILE Gilbert sat in his chair by the window, and while the boys were making a noisy hum all about him, the door opened and Ray Hunter entered with a stranger. The Captain's face was turned away, so that he noticed nothing unusual till he heard Ray say, in the hush which followed his appearance, " Boys, this is Philip Gates, — a new fellow in our class." Then he turned about to look.

The new-comer was as tall as Gilbert himself, had a strong and sturdy figure and a rather handsome face. He did not seem at all abashed at the sight of so many eyes bent upon him, and shook hands with his new acquaintances quite as much at his ease as if it were the hundredth time instead of the first.

The boys were rather cool toward the new-comer. There had not been an addition to their class in a long time, and they were decidedly averse to it; but if he noticed this, he minded it not a whit, and was as affable and pleasant as could be imagined. And when he had been introduced to his new friends, Ray came around with him to where Gilbert sat.

"This is our captain, Gilbert Starr," said he, not without some pride in his tone, — for they all thought they had reason to be proud of him that day, — " and he's head-boy of the school," added Ray, in a whisper.

Philip Gates shook Gilbert's hand, and

as the two stood side by side, Ray noted, with a dim, half-conscious foreboding, that they were just of a height and well-matched.

"I don't see how we can have two such fine fellows in one school," thought he; "they can't both rule, and I wonder if Gates will be contented under Gilbert? He'll have to be, though; there's only one way for him!"

Then the stranger went off to see to his trunk, leaving the boys to discuss his appearance, and surmise what "sort of a fellow he'll be, and whether he can handle an oar, or whether he's worth a snap at cricket."

"But how do *you* like him, Gil?" said Ray, coming back to Gilbert's chair; "he's tall and strong like yourself, and just a match, I should think. And he talks like a jolly fellow, but — but I'm sorry he's come."

" Why ? "

" Because he's ambitious and proud; you could see that plain enough, and, old fellow, you'll have to look out for your command, if I'm not mistaken."

Gilbert laughed, carelessly.

" I'm not troubled at all," he said; " Gates doesn't look very dangerous, and if he is, why, I must be dangerous too. It would be just a tug to see which should rule, I suppose, and— There's the supper-bell, and supper's a great deal better than talk just now, so let's go down."

Gates had a chair at the table next Gilbert's own, and Gilbert was very polite and attentive to him, as it became the head-boy of school to be to a stranger. And as everybody wished to please the Captain that evening, the new-comer re-

ceived more kindness and attention than
he would otherwise have done.

After tea, as they were coming out of
the supper-room, Mrs. Winterhalter met
Gilbert and drew him aside, saying,—

"It's the old trouble about room again.
Another new boy, and nowhere to put him.
But there's only one way to do. He will
have to go in with one of you, and who
shall it be?"

Gilbert's face said, not him; his tongue,
"I don't know, I'm sure. Perhaps, though
I don't know, the boys would rather cast
lots, if he has got to come into our room.
They'll grumble some, I suppose."

"Yes, I know, and so I would rather
you'd settle it among yourselves. May I
leave that to you?"

Gilbert assented, and after Mrs. Winterhalter had detained him awhile to talk
about the day's events and Perry Kent, he

went up to the chamber where most of the class had congregated. Gates was in Mr. Winterhalter's study, undergoing examination. There was great murmuring when he disclosed the fact that some one had got to give up half his bed, and a great deal of wishing that Phil Gates was a thousand miles away.

"But as he isn't," said Gilbert, "and there is a prospect of his being up here in a few minutes, I propose that we cast lots and get through with the business before he returns."

As there was no help for it, lots were drawn. Everybody had a blank but Ray; on his was written "Gates." The boys were jubilant; Ray vexed.

"I declare," said he, "I won't have a bedfellow! I'll sleep on the floor first. I think it's real shabby in Winterhalter, anyhow, that he crowds us so. I've been here three years, and now I've got to give up to the first fellow that comes along."

" But, Ray," said Gilbert, " you know you agreed to go according to the lot."

" Yes, and I will.  Gates shall have my bed,—the whole of it.   I'll sleep on the floor, or hang myself on a hook, I'm not particular which.  And —"

"Perhaps I shall have a word to say in the disposal," said a voice in the door-way, and there stood Gates himself.

Ray flushed a little, but was resolute. The new-comer walked up to the table, looked at the slips of paper, and said, a trifle scornfully, —

" So you've been disposing of me by lot, and Hunter has been the unfortunate one. Well, what's to be done?"

" You're to have the bed," said Ray, shortly.

"But supposing I won't have it?"

"Then it will stay empty."

Now all this was very foolish and silly; but from words they went almost to blows, and all about a bed.    However, Gilbert stepped between them, commanded Ray, entreated Gates, and so forced peace; but from that time the new-comer secretly spited him for this interference, and in due time showed his dislike.    The matter ended by Ray sharing Gilbert's bed, and so all went smoothly again for a time.

The next day was the Sabbath.    There was the usual walk to church and back at noon; the Sunday lunch of bread and milk, and the scattering of the boys in all directions to spend the remainder of the day. Gilbert and Ray came down from a long talk in their room, and found Perry Kent out on the piazza, — quite pale, but better.    Ray stopped, out of courtesy, to give the boy a few sympathizing words, then passed on; but Gilbert lingered. He was thinking of another Sunday, when he found his protege with a Bible, and was not quite sure but there was one out of sight somewhere among the cushions of the easy-chair in which he sat.

"And now what are you thinking about?" he asked of Perry, after he had leaned a long time in silence against one of the pillars of the piazza, busy with his own thoughts.

"About you," said his protege, "and about yesterday afternoon when I saw you enter the study. And then I was thinking about the tumble into the river, and how everybody says you risked your life to save me. I didn't think then, I was so confused, but I forgot to thank you."

A half-smile played about the corners of Gilbert's mouth, and then his face grew very grave.  "Do you think you are very deeply in debt to me?" he asked.

Perry answered, "More than I can ever pay," and said it so earnestly that Gilbert turned away his face, — to look at the river, he pretended.

He sat down by his protege presently, saying, "Do you know I feel as if I could never forgive myself, nor be forgiven, for all that's happened in these weeks?  And, you see, if you had drowned and I discovered that you were — were not what I thought you, why, I should have been miserable all my life for wronging you; and now that you're safe I can't be too thankful, and don't think of the risk."

Perry looked down at the floor, glad and happy.

"And," continued Gilbert, "I don't want you to remember those cruel words I said to you. I'd give a great deal if I might only take them back!"

"You have taken them back,—now, yesterday, and I don't think anything about them. But, but—"

"Go on; don't be afraid," said the Captain.

"But there was one thing —you know— you said that you —you—oh, Gilbert!— you'd never believe in anything good as long as you lived."

Gilbert remembered, and was silent.

"And," continued his protege, "I thought you were just ready to begin and try to do better, and then came the trouble, and you went clear back again, and said — said that."

"Yes, I know," said the Captain; "it shocked me terribly. I didn't know which way to turn, and I thought there was no use trying to be better. I was so miserable —

oh, you don't know, Perry!  But," he added, softly, "I think I would like those words taken back too."

"Oh! would you?" said his protege, delightedly, and then sat looking at Gilbert so thoughtfully that the Captain smiled.

"What are you going to do here all the afternoon by yourself?" he asked.

"Read, and look at the river down below, and think, I suppose; and somehow the time gets away before I know it, and it is night again."

Ray called Gilbert just here, — called to him to come down to the lawn gate where he was standing.

"Isn't there something I can do for you first?" he asked of Perry as he took two or three steps toward obeying Ray's call.

The boy hesitated, looked up to Gilbert's eyes, as if to see how much he might venture to ask, and then said, slowly and with some confusion, "Perhaps you — I wish you would stay and — and read with me."

"Read. what?" Gilbert asked, without showing any annoyance.

"The Bible."

"Aloud to you?"

"Yes, — if you will. Oh, Gilbert! if you only *would*. Don't get angry, but I —"

"Pshaw! I'm not angry. Do you think I fly into a passion at everything? I don't wonder if you do, though. But — where is the Bible?"

Perry's face glowed with a happy smile as he drew out mamma's Bible from some depth of his chair. "Here it is," he said, stroking its brown covers reverently, "and this was mamma's, and here is where her fingers have worn it, and here are her marks, and — and — oh, Gilbert! I do wish you could have seen her!"

Gilbert wished so too.  He took the book with a feeling akin to awe.  Perhaps the memory of that mother's love and gentleness, which so lingered about it and filled Perry's heart, touched his own a little.

"I had a mother once," he said, looking down soberly at the brown covers, "but it was such a long, long time ago that I can only remember the way she used to kiss me. If she had lived — well, I should have been a different fellow, I suppose."

Perry laid his hand on Gilbert's shoulder sympathizingly.  It seemed so strange to hear such words from his lips, and so curious that he should only remember so little of his mother.

"Now," said Gilbert, opening the book, "where shall I read?"

"Wherever you like."

The Captain turned over the leaves a long time, till he had got to the New Testament.

and then stopped to read in St. John. He was a good reader, and Perry had always loved to hear him in the recitations; but now, when the words were so dear and familiar, and there hung about them the double charm of their own purity and mamma's love, mingled with the happy consciousness that it was Gilbert who read them, they had never seemed so beautiful as in the sweet Sabbath stillness of this hour.

At the end of the first chapter, the reader stopped, looked at his listener and found him waiting, and then went on. Gates and some of the Boat Club sauntered around by the syringas, and sat down on the turf. They saw Gilbert and his protege, wondered "if the Cap'n was getting out his translations, or what?" and, after a time, moved on down the lawn. Still Gilbert read, and still Perry listened, delightedly.

By and by, Ray, finding that his friend

failed to answer his call, grew vexed, and, after loitering all about the lawn, drew slowly near the piazza, too independent to hurry, yet wondering what book Gilbert had found so interesting, and feeling secretly jealous of Perry Kent. Finding that the reader did not look up at his approach, he drew softly near, and, at last, went and sat down at his feet on the piazza-steps. With his arms across Gilbert's knees, and his head under his book, he peered up at Perry Kent's rapt face, wonderingly.

"I wonder why Gilbert will let himself be tied up to that pale-faced chit?" he thought to himself, and was vexed.

But Gilbert read on, clear and unfaltering, and Perry listened contentedly, and Ray — frowned ; till Mrs. Winterhalter came out of her parlor to say that Perry must go in.  Then the Captain gave up the

Bible, and his listener was wheeled away, looking back his thanks and love, and then Gilbert turned to Ray.

"You called me," he said, "and I heard; but this little fellow wanted me to read. So I stayed, for which I humbly crave pardon."

Ray looked up, sorrowfully.

"You're just going straight back to your old notions," he said, "and that'll be the end of you. Oh, Gilbert, why can't you take my advice?" shaking his head warningly.

"About what?"

"Why, about—about your notions. You've been reading the Bible a whole hour at least, and if the fellows knew—if they had happened to hear!"

"What then?" coolly.

"You know!—they'd have turned on you at once. If you will and must do such things, what's the use of letting everybody see and know?"

Gilbert's face flushed.

" Ray," said he, " in the first place, I've a perfect right to read any book I choose; and has it harmed me to read the Bible? or where *is* the disgrace?   If it had been Roman history, or a novel, or any of the school-books, you wouldn't have minded a whit; but because it is a better book,— you don't deny that,— you're troubled at once.   I don't see, I *can't* see, how you make out your case!"

" But it looks so priggish and sanctimonious!" persisted Ray.

" Oh, that's the trouble!  Well, I didn't know I was a prig befo—".

" You're not!" said Ray, quickly; " I'd like to see the fellow that'd call you that. But, you see, if a fellow reads the Bible and says his prayers, it looks as if he was trying to set up for a Puritan, and one *can't* be good in school without getting laughed at!"

"Ray," Gilbert exclaimed, with actually a quiver in his voice, "that's just what troubles me! I *do* want to be a better fellow, — I've confessed you that before, — but how to be one without appearing to set up for a prig and a — a — goody sort of a fellow!—oh, can't one do right and still be a man?"

Ray stroked Gilbert's hand with his own, looking exceedingly distressed and uncomfortable. At last he said, —

"I see just how it will be, —I've seen it all along! You'll get into trouble with your new notions, — trouble with the boys, I mean, — and then they'll throw you overboard. They'll pull you down from your rank, and keep you under; and oh, how *can* you ever bear that, and how can I bear to see you there?"

"Always worrying about me!" said Gilbert, smiling; "but never fear, I'll keep my rank, I think; and even if they should bring me down for no other reason than because I want to be a truer fellow—why, I could bear it, I guess. At any rate, I hope I shall have the courage to try. Oh, Ray, can't you give me a help?"

"No; I'm no good in that direction," said he, disconsolately, "and — and — you-'ve got a tough row, old fellow, and I wish you were well through with it; and I'm sure I don't know what's to become of you!" and with this Ray looked ready to cry, if such a thought were to be entertained for a moment by a fellow of his size!

Gilbert laughed cheerily, put his arm about his friend's shoulder, and told him to come with him,—down to the hedge, under the old ash, or anywhere to shake off such heavy spirits,—and leave the future to take care of itself; which Ray did for the rest of Sunday afternoon.

Waning summer fled, and the first fall month came. Asters purpled the road-sides, golden-rod stood up regal and grand in the scrubby fences, and the hills grew soft and yellow; and the crickets chirped noisily in the cool evenings, and earth and sky seemed always whispering that the summer was dead, and winter coming. No days of summer like these,—so full of soft and hazy splendor, breathing such gentle calm and fragrance, slipping by one after another to all the dead days past, leaving only the charm of their memory. Musky, purple, and heavy the grapes hung in the woods; the hazel-nuts drooped their clustered heads, waiting for a gatherer, and when a short one-week vacation came, if nuts and fruits were not all stripped and plundered, it was not the fault of the Rainford boys.

# CHAPTER XVI.

## REBELLION.

ALL these happy days did not go by
without a great many sober thoughts
in Gilbert's heart, — earnest thoughts about
his own way, and much questioning as to
whether he was right, and whether he
could stand against the tide of school opinion which would sweep against him, if he
dared to step out of the beaten way. Ray
Hunter, keen and watchful, fathomed his
friend's thoughts, and was distressed and
perplexed in consequence; and then he
was quite sure that Gates was secretly undermining, and pretty soon, he thought,

down Gilbert would come with the crash which he had predicted. And at last Gilbert's wavering came to an end, and so it came about that one night he knelt down at the foot of his bed and said his prayers before them all. They were all merry and boisterous, and did not notice at first; but when they did, a sudden silence fell upon them. Never were boys more astonished and perplexed. They looked at each other, then at Gilbert, and seemed to doubt their own eyes. Ray Hunter turned away his face to the wall. Gates, who was sitting at the writing-table, turned about to see what the sudden hush meant, and when he comprehended the whole, looked at the boys and laughed audibly. This was the only ridicule to which any expression was given, the others being too much astonished and sobered to laugh or jest about the matter. And when they relapsed again into whispers and undertones, Gilbert had finished and got up to find all his friends looking askance at him over each other's shoulders, apparently regarding him as suddenly removed a long way from themselves.

Without doubt they all regarded him as having done something weak and unmanly, — actually getting down on his knees, — he, Captain Gilbert Starr, — and praying like Perry Kent or any other little fellow just from his mother's apron-strings! This was what they thought, if they did not express it. As if a boy, young, heedless, eager, assailed on every side by temptations, could walk alone unharmed! As if it were not a blessed privilege to ask God's help, and have his great hand guiding, sustaining, comforting, and holding up over the roughness and the snares and pits which are in every boy's path! Weak and unmanly? They were the weak ones who tried to go alone, — stumbling and blinded; they the unmanly who were afraid to own God's love, ashamed to ask his guidance, and trying to creep and cringe along after their own way.

Gilbert's cheeks flushed a little at the sight of so many eyes upon him, and at Gates's prolonged stare; then he threw off his clothes and went to bed.

Gates stopped writing; the boys went to bed one after another, — Ray last of all, without his usual good-night to Gilbert as he got in beside him, — and then the lamp was out, and the room settled down to peace and quietness, save the cricket, who, under the door, made dry, sharp music.

Gilbert lay in the silence, awake and thoughtful. He was thinking most of that deception, a long way back, by which they had won the prize-flag. The thought of it

had rankled in his heart day after day
since there had been truer, more earnest
thoughts there; and now he wished and
longed that there was some way by which
he might undo the whole deception,—tell
Mr. Winterhalter all, perhaps, and, though
that would disclose his own deceit, it
would end the feeling of meanness and
shame which he felt whenever the pennon
fluttered above him. Maybe it was late in
the day to be stirring about it, but the deception grew no better by being older, he
thought. But how to do it? Of course the
Club must know, and they would be furious,
he well knew. It might even cost him his
rank, and Mr. Winterhalter might think
fit to disgrace them all. In that case his
men would lay all the blame upon him,
and—well, the prospect rather disheart-
ened him. It was not pleasant to think
of all his friends as enemies, and Mr.

Winterhalter stern and severe. And his evil act was a very thoughtless one; he did not think of the evil which lay behind it when his lips proposed it. It was done hastily, and the risk of detection seemed then only a pleasant excitement. All these things he thought of, pondered over. There really seemed but one right and manly way to him. But oh, the consequences! So he wavered, hesitated, and after a long struggle decided. He would tell Mr. Winterhalter all in the morning. Come disgrace or blame, that would be the right way, he thought, and the Right Way was the one he was trying to follow. After the battle was over and his decision made, it did not seem so hard; yet he could not but surmise what his men would say. He dreaded their censure a little,—yes, a good deal; more than he was willing to own, perhaps.

In the silence he heard Ray's soft breathing as he slumbered beside him, and thought, gratefully, "Dear old fellow! he'll stand by me, if the rest don't. He likes the right a great deal better than he pretends, and I'll have one friend left among them all." And comforting himself somewhat with this, he went to sleep.

He did not awake the next morning till half the boys were up and dressed, Gates and Ray included. The other half were awake, loitering and lounging sleepily at their toilets. His heart beat rather quick and fast as he turned from the glass after combing his hair, saying, —

"Boys, I've got something I want to say to you. Will you listen a minute?"

"As long as you like, Cap'n," said Tom Fowler, good-humoredly, and the rest hushed their clamor.

Ray stood with towel in one hand and

soap in the other, looking at his friend with a foreboding face. Then Gilbert said,—

"You remember the prize-flag, boys? I—"

"Of course we do," interrupted Tom. "What's coming now?"

"Just this: I've felt mean and ashamed ever since—since a little after we won it. It wasn't won fairly, you all know, and I'm to blame for it because I proposed the plan; and I can't feel right or honorable till I've settled it. So I'm going to tell Mr. Winterhalter the whole, and—"

An indignant, excited buzz, mingled with "Shame! shame!" filled the room and drowned the rest.

"Why, that's downright treachery," said Albert Turner, with more passion than any one had ever seen him display before, "and I for one won't stand such an outrageous piece of meanness!"

"Nor I," said Bob Upham, who generally took his opinions at second-hand; "you got us into the trap, and now you're going to betray us."

"No," said Gilbert, his eyes sparkling a little at the epithets; "I shall accuse no one but myself, and will take all the responsibility. I'm most to blame, and will take the disgrace, if there is any."

"That won't do," said Tom, fiercely,—"it won't do at all! I call it all mean and treacherous, and just one of your new-fangled notions about right and duty; and I never knew a fellow set up such preaching without turning traitor, or a prig, or something equally bad!"

This touched Gilbert sorely; but he bit his lips, and managed to hold his temper while the storming went on about him, and grew fiercer and fiercer. Ray had not said a word as yet.

" There's just this about it," said Albert Turner; "it's plain that such treachery won't pass with us. You wouldn't have thought of such a thing three months ago. You wouldn't have insulted us by proposing it; and if you go to Winterhalter with it, I'll—I'll—"

" What?" said Gilbert, calmly.

" Fight you, if the rest don't!" said Turner, hotly.

The boys expected to see Gilbert turn upon the secretary at once, and for a moment he looked as if such were his intentions; then he grew calmer, and said,—

" I shall do it, however. I think it's the only right and honorable way, and if you all fight me, it won't make any difference; and if you won't give your consent, I must do without it."

He had finished dressing while speaking these words, and now moved toward the door. Tom Fowler threw his stout figure against it, defiantly, and several members of the Boat Club rallied about him.

"Let's see you turn traitor!" said Tom, between his teeth. "You can't make your new notions go down here, sir!"

Two bright, angry spots came into Gilbert's cheeks at this, and his hands clinched. He was not used to being either opposed or threatened, you remember.

Ray sprang up, thinking there was going to be trouble, and wondering if it was really best for him to uphold Gilbert's outrageous opinions. But there was no fight. Gilbert simply said,—

"I'm going out of that door, Tom, and do you stand back, or I'll make you;" and upon that Tom's supporters left him, and there was no other way for him but to give up too.  So Gilbert went out unmolested, and stopped a minute in the hall to calm the wild thoughts which this clash with his men had stirred up, and not daring to stop to mourn over the affair, lest his resolution should fail him, went on to the study.

Mr. Winterhalter was there, and answered his rap with a face that betrayed some surprise at this call before breakfast. "But come in, come in, Gilbert," he said; "I'm not very busy, — only a letter or two that won't mind waiting, and I'm always glad to see you."

The Captain secretly doubted whether he could say that, after his story was told, but followed the Principal in and sat down in the chair which he placed beside his writing-desk; and then he was at a loss what to say.

Mr. Winterhalter looked over his letters, up at the clock, askance at his head-boy, and waited. At last, "Mr. Winterhalter!" desperately.

"Well, Gilbert?" wondering what the Captain was so nervous about.

"I—I deceived you a long time ago, sir, and—I'm ashamed and sorry for it. I wish—if you could only forgive me— that—that— Oh, Mr. Winterhalter, I've been very dishonorable!"

The Principal eyed Gilbert keenly, and looked puzzled.

"I don't understand," he said; "you're not dishonorable, Gilbert."

"Oh, but I am—I was!" said he, every word a wound to his pride, and his cheeks glowing as he made this confession; "I deceived you about the flag, Mr. Winterhalter. We—I, I mean, was afraid we should lose it on account of Tom Fowler's lessons, and so I helped him,—wrote them out for him, and got out his problems, and—and so got the flag that way."

A long silence followed, in which Gilbert did not look up once, thinking, in the depth of his humiliation, that deceit and dishonor led their followers a hard, hard way. Then, "But weren't the rest of the class knowing to this, sir?"

"Y—e—s," Gilbert confessed; "but it was I who proposed it, and I who carried it along, and—and I want to bear all the blame, sir."

"Do the rest agree to that?"

"N—n—o, perhaps not; I believe they are not agreed at all, sir."

Another long silence. Then Mr. Winterhalter got up, came to Gilbert, and looked straight into his eyes for a few seconds before he said,—

"One more question.  Did the boys oppose your making a confession of this?"

" A—little."

The principal looked down at him, his
face softening more and more as he looked.
At last he said,—

"I was disappointed in you, Gilbert,
but—but you're an honest fellow, and I'm
proud of that.  And, my dear boy, I think
I know something of the struggle you've
been through, and what you are striving
for, and what you will have to meet; and
do you think I can talk about blame or
disgrace?  No; it's the farthest thing from
my heart; and if you always show yourself as noble as you have this morning,
why—why—Gilbert, give me your hand,"
said Mr. Winterhalter.

Gilbert was surprised; his face showed
that, and he was touched by these kind
words, and so, perhaps, he was not sorry

that the breakfast-bell rang just then and gave him an opportunity to slip away, even though it prevented him from hearing what the Principal would have said further.

None of his friends spoke to him at the breakfast-table, and it was rather a silent meal for all; and when it was over, the Boat Club disappeared and left him there alone. Of course this hurt Gilbert somewhat, though he did not show it. "They-'ll feel better-natured soon," he thought; "especially when they find there's no harm to come to them from what I've done;" and so he lingered there by himself, wondering what had become of Ray. A half-hour passed, then another, and then Perry came in.

"Oh, here you are!" he exclaimed; "I've been searching everywhere for you, Gilbert. And do you know they're terribly angry at you up-stairs? But you won't mind, will you? Gates and Albert Turner talked— But they wouldn't let me stay, and sent me to give you this."

Gilbert took the little note and opened it, while Perry watched his face to see what its purport might be. This was what the Captain read:—

"GILBERT STARR,—The Boat Club would like to see you in their room a few minutes, on business.     ALBERT TURNER."

He crumpled it up in his hand, hesitated a few seconds, and finally went. He walked into the chamber to find all his class assembled,— Albert Turner at the writing-table, the rest scattered about in the chairs and on the foot of their beds. As cool and quiet as ever, he looked at the lowering faces a second, and then sat down on his own bed, waiting to see what was wanted of him.

 The secretary fidgeted about in his chair, and looked at Tom and Gates uneasily, then at Bob and Barry, and failing to make himself understood, exclaimed impatiently,—

"Come, who's to be spokesman?"

No one stirred at first, then Tom got up, saying, in his clumsy way,—

" Well, I 'spose it might be said first as last, even if it's me that blunders it out. The truth is, we've got tired of your rule, Starr, and we think the Club might have a better captain. You've been kind of dropping off from what you used to be, and when a fellow gets so that he turns traitor to his own men, we'd like to be excused from training in the same company."

Gilbert's face flushed crimson, his eyes

began to blaze, and he got up with the old fiery spirit within him.

"Tom, you sha'n't talk so to me!" he exclaimed. "What do you think I'll bear? Not *that*, I can tell you!" and he took Tom by the shoulders as if he intended to give him a shaking; but he remembered himself presently, and turned away, saying, "It isn't worth fighting about, but I won't hear any more. Now, Turner, what do you want of me?"

"Tom has told you," said the secretary, curtly.

"Well, do you mean that you want me to resign, or that you rebel, or what?" the Captain asked.

"We mean both," said Tom. "If you won't resign, we'll rebel. We won't serve under you, anyhow."

Gilbert's pride was roused. His men talking to him like that! his men threatening rebellion! his men calling him traitor!

"You know," he said, proudly, "that you can't force me out. You put me in this place for as long as I am in school. The head-boy always has it;" then he was sorry for the words as soon as they were spoken, for who could wish to stay where he was hated? "Stop!" he exclaimed; "I don't mean that. I don't wish the place, if you feel so. Do you speak for them all, Tom Fowler?"

Now Gilbert certainly thought Ray would stand by him. He expected it; looked to see him cry out in his eager, impetuous way, when he asked this question; but instead, he averted his face and was silent. And this was the keenest cut which he had felt.

"Yes," said Tom; "I speak for them all. If any disagree, let 'em speak out."

There was a significant silence,. during which Gilbert's cheeks slowly reddened and paled at the thought of all his friends deserting him so; then he said, gravely, "I resign my place," and went out.

"I declare, I'm glad it's over!" said Tom, as the door closed; "it comes kind o' hard to put the old fellow out of his place in that fashion.  He feels it, you may be sure."

"Now don't *you* go to turning chicken-hearted," said the secretary.

"Don't you bother! I ain't made of stone, as you are, but I can manage, I guess."

Ray got up, thinking, "It's come, just as I said; and oh, I wish—I wish I had stuck to him through thick and thin! But he deserves it, anyhow, the obstinate fellow! and— Poor old fellow!"

# CHAPTER XVII.

## HOW HE ENDURED IT.

FOR a boy who had always ruled, and ruled strongly,— for one accustomed to be looked to as the head of the school, the arbitrator of all disputes and quarrels, the boy-authority from whom there was no appeal, this was a great tumble. True, he was head-boy still, because he ranked highest in the highest class, but with his command taken away, his men all denouncing and disowning him, his honor pronounced to be *dis*honor by his former friends, and all his good qualities a sham, Gilbert suddenly found himself without influence or authority.

This discovery shocked him a little at first, then he resolutely set about accustoming himself to the new phase of affairs. "It *is* as Ray prophesied," he said to himself; "but I can endure it I guess, for I'm sure I'm right. Who'd have thought it would come to this ? and that Ray would desert me?— and all—just all of it — because I chose to do what seemed right!"

You may surmise who took Gilbert's place. It was Philip Gates. Albert Turner made a short struggle for the position, but the new-comer, in some mysterious manner, got the most votes, and from thenceforth was Captain Philip Gates. Ray Hunter, with a little striving, might have secured the honor, but he said, "I'd sooner go and hang myself than try to fill Gilbert Starr's place. Gates may have it, if he wants it, — he's welcome. For my part, I prefer private life at present."

Tom Fowler said, "Catch *me* in that place? No, sir! it would look too much as if I had been undermining in order to step into the Captain's shoes. Yes, let Gates have it if he wants it; he's welcome enough, I'm sure."

So Gates had it, and his first act was to persuade them all to "cut" Gilbert, which they did. Gilbert did not appear to mind this very much, though it was rather awkward at first to sit at the table amid all the merry chatter and talk, without being spoken to or noticed in any way. And at this juncture he began to miss Ray's sprightly tongue and cheery presence sadly. The two often met in the hall, or at recitations, and sometimes even read off the same book; but Ray's face was always cold, disdainful, and unyielding,— belying his heart, Gilbert was sure. Of course this state of affairs speedily made itself known to the Winterhalters.　The good lady met Gilbert in the hall one day, took his hand and said, all the while looking kindly into his eyes, "We know all about it, dear, — the whole story.　You mustn't ask me how I found out, but 'twas half an accident; and we are happier over it than anything you ever did before.　Mr. Winterhalter says, 'Gilbert's enduring for the sake of the right and the true, and when he comes out of the trouble, he'll be stronger and more faithful to himself and God.'　And that's what I think."

"But — but, do you think I shall ever come out?" he asked, showing the first signs of depression which he had ever exhibited. He was in sombre spirits that day, and the boys had annoyed him in a hundred petty ways, till his resolution gave away a little and let out those words.

"Ever come out of the trouble?" said she, her motherly eyes opening wide; "why,

to be sure you will! Right always tri-
umphs, — always.   It may not be to-day
nor to-morrow, in one year or a score,
but at last it gains the Victory.   And so
with you, — a month may not bring the end,
nor this term, perhaps, but that it will come
and come happily, you may believe."

"I haven't a friend in school, except Perry
Kent," said Gilbert, with just a trace of
sadness in his eyes.

"Has Ray forsaken you?" asked Mrs.
Winterhalter, quickly.

Gilbert's grave "Yes," almost a sigh,
showed how keenly he felt this desertion.

"Well, it *is* a hard thing to lose all one's
friends and one's dearest friend at once,"
said she, kindly; "but I think you made
up your mind for anything that might happen when you started, didn't you?"

"Not for that!" said he.

"But take heart!" said Mrs. Winterhalter; "you and Ray can't be enemies more than a month at one time. I predict that!" said she, smiling; " and now, if there were not such a great basket of mending waiting for me in the parlor, I would stay and talk longer, but as there is I must go on. But when you're lonesome or discouraged, come into the parlor, — at any time, — you know the way, Gilbert!" The good lady left a little streak of sunshine behind her to gladden his way for the rest of the day; and most days he was generally cheerful and light-hearted enough.

Day after day went by, Gilbert shut out by his class from all their sports and plans, passed by, overlooked. There was Perry Kent left, and that was all. It was not strange that in this long and wearisome state of affairs he should find the little boy good company, and think him a great comfort; and that the little fellow in return clung closer than ever to his big friend. The friendship between them was something pleasant to see, — Perry always eager and anxious to shield his protector from the idle talk and stories which floated about school, and grated so on Gilbert's feelings when he heard them; and so, when some malicious member of the Boat Club would whisper a sneering thing about their old Captain into his ears, hoping it would be repeated and hit the mark at which it was shot, he wisely and kindly let it go no further, and Gilbert was left undisturbed. Not many of the Club would stoop to this way of wounding their enemy, but a few endeavored to do it more than once, meeting, thanks to Gilbert's protege, with but very indifferent success.

And did they not miss him all this time? Yes; and at first very sorely, though nothing could tempt them to own it, of course.

Gates's rule was vastly different from Gilbert's, and some of them secretly chafed
under it; and Gates himself was a very
different youth.  In his uniform he looked
as finely as the old Captain, though maybe not quite so erect, and he could handle an oar tolerably, "but—but—" as Tom
Fowler secretly confessed to Ray, as they
walked up from the boat-house one evening after practice, "he's no more like our
t'other Cap'n than—than I am."

"Well, you don't want him to be, I
suppose," said Ray; "that wouldn't suit
you at all."

"Not *just* like him, to be sure," Tom
said, "but something like.   Gilbert Starr
beat everything at being Captain."

"Wouldn't you have him back now, if
you could?" Ray asked, quietly.

"Not I!" his wrath blazing up fiercely.
"He's set himself up for a pious, preach-

ing old deacon, and he may have it all to himself. Gilbert Starr is a treacherous, sne —"

Ray's hand went over Tom's mouth, much to that young gentleman's astonishment and indignation.

"What did you mean?" he demanded.

"Gilbert's my friend," the other answered, simply.

"Goodness gracious! now you're fibbing it, Hunter! Why, you're the coldest towards him of any of us!" cried Tom.

"I know it," Ray answered, remorsefully; "but I don't mean a bit of it. Oh, Tom Fowler, I'm the miserablest fellow in Rainford town!"

"You must be, if you're spooneying over Gilbert Starr. But, confound it! why don't you kick the traces and get free? *I* would, if I felt like that."

"So would I — if I could," said Ray.

There was a trace of frost in the air, and the rest of the boaters came running up behind them, and from thence they raced up to the house to get warm. Gilbert sat on the piazza in the dusk, the Club all brushing by him in silence and with averted eyes up to their room, Ray as grim as any of them.

"Well, you *are* the queerest chap," whispered Tom to him, as they came together on the stairs; "I couldn't have done that, if I felt as you do, to have saved my neck. With me, it's act just as you feel; I can't help it no more than breathing. But you! Oh, Ray Hunter, you're the strangest mixture!"

"I know—I'm lying all the time; but —but—"

The clamor in the hall drowned the rest of it, and Tom's curiosity was not great enough to lead him to say more on the subject; but it was quite certain that Ray was, as he said, the most miserable fellow in Rainford town.

But what Gilbert lost in one way was made up to him in others. He had nearly twice as much time to himself as before, and now his studies began to flourish vigorously. When he was Captain Starr, his time was so taken up by boating and all the trifling matters of sports and summer pleasures, that books were almost a secondary matter, and he had only studied enough to get the day's lessons and keep his rank. Now there were mornings and evenings all to himself, or with no one by but Perry, and, somehow, he was never an interruption; and in consequence, he began to go on and up, distancing his companions who had still games and boat-practice to employ their attention.

But all pleasures were not quite given

up, though they were to be enjoyed almost alone. He chanced to remember, one Saturday afternoon, that Perry Kent had never taken a sail upon the river.

"I don't believe there's another boy in school can say the same," Gilbert thought to himself; "and I'll just go and give him a good float down-stream. It will do me good, too, and the river looks its prettiest now."

He put away the books which he had been conning, got his cap and rowing-jacket, and went in search of his protege.

Perry was all by himself in a far corner of the lawn, the other boys having taken themselves either to the river or woods.

"And why didn't you go too?" Gilbert asked, when he found him there.

The boy evaded the question as long as possible, till his protector forced him to reveal his reason; and then it came out that they had refused to let him accompany them because "you're just one of Gilbert Starr's friends, and if you stick to him, you may stay with him; we won't have you," as they said.

Gilbert bit his lips, saying, almost bitterly,—

"Anything that I have to do with suffers. Why don't you renounce me, Perry, and go over to the other side?"

"*You?* because I can't,—I wouldn't for the whole world, Gilbert."

The ex-Captain smiled a little, and said, at last,—

"Well, if everybody has gone off to spend the afternoon, we might as well go too; though it makes little difference whether we go or stay, so far as they are concerned. Wouldn't you like a sail, Perry?"

" A sail, and with you, Gilbert? · Oh, yes !"

" Then come down to the wharf, and if there's any boats left, we'll go down the river a ways. It's just the day for a row, —so cool and bright, and the river never'll look prettier, for the trees begin to fade already. Pretty soon it will be cold weather, and then good-by to boating for this year. Well, we've had some good races, anyhow," said Gilbert, with something like a sigh.

Down the slope they went in silence, the grasshoppers flying up in little droves before their feet, as they brushed the dry and rustling grass. The sunshine was warm and pleasant everywhere, and over all the land there was such peace and quiet as only October's fair and golden days can bring.

"How still it is!" said Perry,—"just like Sunday."

There was one boat secured at the old wharf-post,—a little skiff, rising and falling with the ripples,—and into this they got and Gilbert cast off.

"The 'Triton' is gone," he said, as they pushed out beside the boat-house, "and the Club must be on the river somewhere." He worked his boat out to the mid-channel, and then allowed it to drop down-stream with the slow current. What a bright afternoon it was!—so much fairer out there on the river, with the great blue cloudless arch above, and the great blue dimpling flood beneath, heaving and swelling and bearing them down on the throbs of its bosom. Gilbert threw off his cap, shook back his hair in the steady puffs of breeze that made the river their highway, and looking at the little boy in the stern, said, with one of his cheery old smiles, " This is like life once more! Somehow, it makes a new fellow of me, as if all my troubles flew away with the breeze; and oh, I wish we had nothing to do but go on and on, down to the sea."

The river-bank flitted by, gay with many-hued asters, crimson-leaved creepers, the yellow drapery of grape-vines, with here and there the deep green of a cedar thrusting up its tapering head through the brilliant tangle of bush and vine. Wherever there was room in the shallows, the grass waved and rustled, still rank, and vivid in hue as ever. Before them the river spread wide and far till it hid itself between the hills below, — the hills that glowed softly with their wealth of red and yellow, sober russet, tawny orange, and marone all blended by distance into rich, subdued color; behind them lay Riverside with its roofs and towers mirrored in the dancing tide below.

"How pleasant!—how beautiful!" said Perry, drawing in long breaths as he gazed. "Oh, Gilbert isn't this the loveliest place you ever saw?"

"Yes, *I* think so, always; it's all the home I've got, you see, so that it's *home* to me, with all the rest of the brightness added."

"And we're getting 'way down till Mr. Winterhalter's meadows have almost faded out. It doesn't take long to come on this current."

"No," said Gilbert, turning the boat's head a little; "we're a good way from home already. We'll go in toward shore a little. Look at the grape-vines, Perry! I wonder if there are any frost-grapes left? We can look, at any rate."

A little while after, the boat's prow ran

in under the luxuriant growth of vine and willows, mingled with alders and thinly-scattered maples, most of them robbed of their flaming robes, and here Gilbert fastened the boat, saying, —

" Now for frost-grapes !　They're here as thick as — as — I don't know what.　I wonder why Roth's boys haven't found them before?　Just look over your head, Perry Kent!"　The leaves were so few and thin that Perry could see the grapes — small, black things — hanging in the greatest profusion.　" They need just a smart touch of frost to make 'em good," said Gilbert, throwing down a quantity, " and they've had it.　Do you like them?"

Before his protege could answer, there was a rustling and crashing of steps in the underbrush, and then a tall figure pushed through, — in search of grapes, too, it was evident.

" Forrest ! " exclaimed Gilbert.

" Gilbert Starr ! " cried the new-comer.

" Well, I was just wondering why your school hadn't found these," said Gilbert, pleasantly.

" And I've been waiting a whole week for this afternoon," said Captain Forrest. " My men wanted to be on the river, but I sent 'em off alone and came down here afoot —"

" To find me eating your grapes ! " smiled Gilbert.

" No, there's enough, I hope ! and I'd rather see you than the grapes, a hundred times. How are you, Starr, and why don't you ever come over to Riverside to see me ? " Forrest had professed a great liking for Gilbert since the rescue at the boat race.

Gilbert pulled down a long, swaying

branch, dark with fruit, and said, after a little pause, —

" Don't you know? — haven't you heard? I've resigned my place, and my men cut me a long time ago."

" Yes, I knew you weren't Captain, but I didn't know they'd cut you! Why, what do they mean, and what happened?" Here Forrest spied the boat and Perry, and got into it, saying, " Come, sit down, Starr. You've got grapes enough on that branch for us all, and I want to know how you got into such trouble."

Gilbert followed him, not at all inclined to reveal the cause of his trouble, which the other perceived, and added, politely, —

" Oh, never mind about it, if you don't wish to. I thought perhaps you'd just as lief as not."

" It was about our prize-flag," said Gilbert, as he sat down; and then he went on

with some of the particulars, his tone getting lower and lower till Perry could not
hear what he said. But his friend's cheeks
were so red, and Forrest gazed so steadfastly
in the water, that he was quite sure Gilbert
was telling his old rival the whole story,
from beginning to end. When he finished,
there was a long silence on their part, but
the river washed and rippled against its
bank, and with a dip and plash of oars the
"Triton" and its crew shot past, coming up
from an excursion down the river. Gilbert looked after them,—his face a little sad,
perhaps, for Forrest took his hand, saying
comfortingly, —

"I can feel for you, old fellow, for don't
I know how it would hurt me to see the
'Mermaid' flying by, and I not even looked
at? I'm no good at consoling a body, but I
*do* feel for you, and I wish you'd let me
be your friend through it all. A fellow

mayn't mind it at first, but when he's cut by everybody for weeks at a time, it's dull and lonesome, anyhow!"

Gilbert thanked him, and when the "Triton" was out of sight, said, —

"It *is* hard to bear, — I don't mind confessing it to you, — but which would *you* do, Forrest, — stick to what you think is right and true, or give up to them?"

"I'm not much at doing what's right and true," he answered, slightly coloring; "but — but I'd stick to my principles, now that I'd got started with 'em."

After another attack on the grape-vine, Gilbert said it was time to go home; so the boat was turned about. They took Forrest with them and carried him back to Riverside, turning from their course to that bank of the river for the purpose.

When the Professor's head-boy landed at

the steps, he turned about and wrung Gilbert's hand, saying,—

"You're right, Starr, and I hope you'll succeed. I do a thousand things myself that I hate and detest, but I *can't* get rid of it. I don't believe I could ever do as you have done; I haven't the courage."

The little wharf was silent and deserted when they got over there, and the "Triton" in its place. Gilbert said, cheerily, as he got out to fasten their little skiff,—

"This has been a pleasant afternoon, and I'll go boating every Saturday till cold weather comes; see if I don't. It makes me feel like a new fellow. Tired, Perry?"

# CHAPTER XVIII.



"MY LESSONS."

THE days went by, and October began to wane. The glory on the hills was dimmed, and began to fade into sombre, chilly nakedness. Yet now and then a bright day shone out, clear and warm as summer, as if Mother Nature's heart relented, and she were half a good mind to keep winter at bay, and let the earth blossom and bask on in warmth and shine. The "Triton" was laid up for the season, and all the little boats along the river-bank disappeared; and since there was no more boating, there was ball-play on the lawn morning and night.

Gilbert Starr applied himself to his books determinedly, and consequently made his way upward in a manner which delighted Mr. Winterhalter vastly. And it was also quite certain that he walked upward in more ways than one; and even his enemies did not deny that. And all unconsciously he began to show, as he walked on day after day, how a boy might be tender and true without being weak; valiant and fearless for the Right, and yet not a prig; fearing and remembering God, yet strong and manly, and a boy still. And since he did this unconsciously, with no thought of what his conduct might be showing to others, it came about, after a time, that some eyes were opened to the fact that Gilbert Starr was not a sham. None of his enemies confessed this; oh, no!—that would have been owning that he was right all the time, and that they had wronged him; but in their secret hearts they knew it, felt it, and owned it; and so respected him accordingly. But did they relent at all? Not a whit. Boys are as obstinate as — anything; and Mr. Winterhalter's were no exception. What! let Gilbert himself, and the whole school, and everybody know that they had wronged him? that he was not a sham and a traitor? that he was real, true, solid gold? No! that would never, never do. Secretly they might own it; openly, not yet, not yet!

But there was one heart in the Boat Club which grew desperate waiting so long, and that, you will readily surmise, was Ray Hunter's. Without the courage at first to break away from his friends and stand up for Gilbert and — as he thought — his outrageous opinions, he had only one choice, and that was, to be numbered among his enemies. Here, of course, he was miserable enough, for the disgraced Captain was as dear to him as was ever one boy to another; and to pass him by, day after day, without a word or look, — to shun him, when he longed so earnestly to be with him, comfort him, help him to bear it all, was as much as he could possibly endure. What was meant as a punishment for Gilbert was the torment of his life. Sometimes he fancied the ex-Captain was sad and suffering under his misfortunes, and then his own heart was heavy and miserable.

" Oh, if I could just help the poor, dear old fellow with it all!" he would exclaim, remorsefully. Again, he would be piqued because Gilbert did not apparently miss him; because he moved on undisturbed, going his own way, and leaving the Club to go theirs. Then he would say, bitterly, " Well, let him keep on!

he hasn't a bit of heart, anyhow, and I can manage without him, I guess."

But he could *not* "manage" without him, and knew it well enough.

It was very awkward, too, at night, when it came time to go to bed, that he must share the same pillow with his friend. He wished, a hundred times, that he had kept his own bed with Gates. But there was no help for it now, and so he was obliged to get in one side, very cool and grim, while Gilbert got in on the other, rather grave and sober, yet not without a trace of a smile on his face, sometimes, it was all so ridiculous. Oh, how many times Ray awoke in the stillness of the night to find his friend sleeping tranquilly beside him, and to wish that he had never put such a great deep gulf between them!

"He doesn't suffer half so much as I do!" he would think at such times; "and he doesn't mind if we have all cut him, and he's just going straight on, farther and farther away from us all, and—and by and by there'll be no catching up with him." Yet for a long, long time he could not bring his mind to the thought of "endorsing" Gilbert's new opinions, and especially his conduct in regard to the prize-flag. And when he found that his friend had evidently taken all the blame upon his own shoulders and that none came back upon the Boat Club,—when he was quite sure of this, and had got over his scruples, then pride and pique held him back. But when October was fleeing so fast, all the days like so many lovely pictures in a wonderful framing, and the first chill breaths floated up the river and over the land, how could he wait longer? It was an utter impossibility to be Gilbert's enemy any longer, and he gave up the thought. But how to be reconciled?

It came about that, as he came in from
playing ball one evening, he found Gilbert
sitting on the piazza, without books or papers, and quite alone.   Here was an opportunity, and he almost stopped; then his courage quite forsook him, and he kept on up
to the chamber, vexed and out of patience
with himself.   But when he had reached
the top of the stairs, he thought, " There
never'll be any better time !   He's all alone,
and it's now, or never !" and turning about,
went slowly back, looking behind to see
that his friends of the Club were not following.   He opened the glass door and stepped out on to the piazza, to find that in his
absence Perry Kent had made his appearance, and was leaning against Gilbert's chair.
A sudden chill of disappointment, not un-
mixed with jealousy, came over him, and he
stopped short.   " I won't go near him !"
he said, bitterly.

It was not many seconds, however, before he remembered that Perry Kent was all
the friend Gilbert had remaining. Whom
else could he talk or chat with?—and who
was to be blamed for it? "I'm a fool!"
he thought, and closed the door behind him.
Gilbert did not hear, Perry did not notice.
They chatted on, merrily, all unconscious
who was watching at the farther end of the
piazza. Ray bit his lips, and paced about
with his hands in his pockets.

In the west a lucent glow, pure and shining, overspread the sky, and against the
amber background Riverside hill, with its
roofs and steeples, stood up, sharp and
clear as a sculpture. There was going to
be an evening-service in the churches, for
just then the bells suddenly struck into a
sweet chiming that floated down as if from
belfries in the clouds. Ray leaned against
a pillar to listen, and as the silvery echoes

rang out across the long dusk shadow through which the river rolled, and came up to his ears in soft and soothing whispers, his heart grew tender and his face wistful. He looked across his shoulder at the two figures, and wished Perry Kent would run away, if for only a minute. When the bells were still, he went on with his pacing, up and down the steps, a little way on the gravel-walk, then back again to the piazza, eager and restless.

Tom Fowler found him here, impatiently walking about, and asked, "What's up now? You act like a parson that's put off his sermon till Saturday night and flies about trying to think it up! May I ask what the text is to be to-morrow?—perhaps I could give you an idea or two."

Ray did not fly into a passion as usual, but said, "Go on with you, Tom! I can't talk with you now."

" But aren't you chilly? "

" It's no matter,—no, I'm warm enough. Go on, Tom! "

Tom went on.

Perry Kent heard voices, looked around, but saw only Ray Hunter walking slowly up and down the farther end of the piazza. He thought little of it then, but by and by, when he chanced to look that way again, he saw the figure still pacing. Then a sudden thought flashed into his mind, only a suspicion at first, but growing into a certainty as he pondered over it. It kept him silent a long while. At last he said, " Gilbert, I guess, perhaps, I'd better go in."

" Why, no, the stars are just coming out ! What are you going 'in for, now?"

" Because, I — I'd better, I guess. You won't mind, Gilbert? And perhaps I'll come back after a while, if you want me to."

Gilbert said, " Well, you're funny ! I

never knew you want to miss the stars coming out, before.  Is it too cold?"

Perry slipped away without much of a
reply, and was not particular to shut the
glass door very softly.

Ray looked around, saw Gilbert alone,
and exclaimed to himself, "Bless Perry
Kent!  I — I really believe he did that on
purpose."

His friend's face was turned away as he
hurried eagerly toward him, he did not notice, did not hear; looking up to the stars
and half leaning against the piazza-rail, he
did not turn till he heard, —

" Gilbert !", chokingly.

" What, Ray?"

There were a few seconds of deep silence,
in which somebody was trying to find his
voice enough to say, " We two can't afford
to be enemies?"

" No!" and their hands claspod.

Something bright and glittering fell on Gilbert's sleeve. Of course Ray was too big to cry, and presently this young gentleman says, with a very husky voice, —

."May I just ask you to—to—to forgive me, old fellow?"

Gilbert put his arm over his friend's shoulder. "Of course!" he said; "don't you suppose I saw—don't you think I knew that you didn't mean it? Oh, Ray!"

"But, Gilbert, it was cruel in me. I—I'm ashamed!—and I was miserable all the time. And if you'll just let me be your friend once more—"

"You are! you were all the time!" said Gilbert, assuringly; "it was hard, sometimes, but I thought it would all come right, if I waited. And I don't believe you and I can help being friends, Ray, whatever happens."

Ray sat down on the arm of his friend's

chair, hiding his face with one hand, while the other still grasped Gilbert's. "I deserted you!" he exclaimed, shame and regret apparent enough in his voice; "and I left you to bear all your troubles alone, and now it don't seem right that you should just take me back the same as if nothing had happened!"

"Why?"

"Because — I've wronged you, and — isn't that enough? Can you ever trust me — as you did before?"

"Trust Ray Hunter?" said Gilbert, with a little laugh; "well, I think I can. I shall try at any rate. Haven't you been the truest of fellows since the first day I came to Rainford school till — till then? And do you think I would cast you off if I could? I don't think you'll leave me again."

"Desert you again!" said Ray; "never,

if you are expelled or banished or — But
I won't make any promises. A fellow
can't tell — he's tempted so sometimes;
and you'll just have to take me as I am."

"I do," said Gilbert.

Ray sat there very silent and very humble, and too happy to say much about it.
Gilbert didn't appear any differently than
ever, he thought, — not at all proud and
above him because of his new opinions,
nor as if he were one whit better than
himself; but just the same dear, frank,
warm-hearted friend, who could forgive a
fellow's faults and failings, and love him
as before. And with this thought in his
heart, he said, falteringly, —

"I thought you were going to be a—
a stiff, priggish, *goody* sort of a fellow
that nobody could like. The Club all said
so; I thought so, too, when you proposed
that plan about the flag. But they know

differently now; so do I." Gilbert was silent. "And I thought another thing. It seemed as if you would get farther and farther off, till you wouldn't have anything to do with such a harum-scarum fellow as I, or the rest of us,— a kind of iceberg toward us all!"

"Well, do I freeze you?" Gilbert asked.

"Freeze me! Oh, I was all wrong about it,— *all* wrong! and if you're a bit farther off, I can't see it, but I feel you're a great deal nearer to *me*. And— But what's the use of talking? You're Gilbert Starr, and that's enough."

The stars were coming out in golden fleets and shining everywhere. The glow in the west was gone, and on Riverside the lights gleamed from hundreds of windows. A boat came up the river, trailing a fiery shadow from the lantern at its prow, and the air was so still that they could just hear the grating of its oars in the rowlocks.

"You know," Ray said, as his eyes followed it, "I did another mean thing. Oh, Gilbert, I'm ready to hide my head when I think of it! I helped to make you resign your place in the Club. If I had spoken out, if I had done as I ought, they might have listened, and you could have kept it, perhaps. And now, oh—"

But Gilbert interrupted, saying,—

"Do you think I would have kept it, Ray? Why, I could not with any honor, after what had been said. And do you think I'm sorry? do you think I care for the place? do you think I would go back to it? No! I *was* sad about it at first, it was such a change for me, you see; but —do you know?—I saw at last why it was best for me to be down where I am now. I never could have been anything

but the dishonest and dishonorable fellow
I was, as long as I stayed there, for the
Club were strongest, and ruled *me*. And
when I got away, or rather when they put
me away, it was just the blessedest thing
they could have done for me. You don't
see how, Ray? Neither did I at first, but
when I look back, it seems to me as if
all the events of this long summer had
been just so many lessons — my lessons —
to teach me some things which I needed
to know very much. And I hope I've
learned some of them."

Ray was silent a long time; then he
said, —

" And you can truly say that you're not
sorry for what you've done?"

" Sorry!" cried Gilbert; " oh, Ray, how
can you ask it? I believe I'm the hap-
piest fellow, now, in Rainford town!"

Some one came up just then, saying, mischievously,—

"Are the stars out yet, Gilbert?"

"Perry Kent!" cried Ray, "give me your hand, you blessed little fellow. Talk about lessons, Gilbert,—why, he's given me one this very night, and I'm not going to forget it."

Up in their towers across the river the bells tolled out heavily for nine, and before their echoes had died away, Mr. Winterhalter's last bell tinkled, and the piazza was empty and deserted.

And those who would follow Gilbert to see whether his feet held steadfast, and where his path led him, whether he failed, or proved victorious, must look for him in another book.